ELUSIVE LIES
by Sebastiaan Fluchard

A d a r k   t r u t h   h i d e s
behind the secrets

Prologue

"Joanne, he's dead!" the man cried out when he heard the front door.

He was crouching beside the body that was lying on the floor between the window and a big wooden desk. Markus had managed to hit the shooter in the neck without even being able to see him.

"What the fuck?!" The man finally looked up and, seeing it was Markus, grabbed the gun and started shooting erratically.

Markus immediately dove back into the hall. He waited behind the wall for what he knew was coming. It was his gun and he had already emptied half the chamber before. Now the man was shooting without restraint. Twelve. Thirteen, fourteen. Fifteen.

Click...Click. The idiot had wasted the last bullets standing between himself and Markus breaking his arms.

Markus slowly walked out from behind the wall. Not in his mind, the man jumped up from the body and launched himself at Markus. It was not what Markus was expecting. The man managed to grab Markus's wounded arm and twisted it behind his back.

Markus gasped and groaned, falling to his knees on the floor. He hadn't been expecting the man to be sharp enough to go straight for that arm. As soon as he realised that his opponent was out for blood and was happy to fight dirty, he decided to do the same. He jabbed his fingers in the man's eyes with as much force as he could muster and gouged at them.

The pain made the creep let go of Markus's arm and he scrambled to the other side of the room, grabbing a vase from the desk to hurl at Markus.

Markus dodged the vase just in time and grabbed a small statue to do the same but instead of waiting to see if it would connect, he hurled himself at the man as well, aiming for where he hoped the man would be as he ducked the projectile. He tackled him to the floor.

Legs straddled over him, he put his cold hands around his throat and squeezed. Markus kept squeezing as the man tried to struggle free. The noises coming out of the man's mouth would have turned the stomachs of most people.

He was near the end. Markus could feel it. The veins in his neck started pulsing and his face was turning purple.

Blood was desperately trying to find a way to his brain but Markus did not let it. He was going to kill him. He was going to kill the creep who had hurt the woman he loved.

– *Five weeks earlier* –

When Markus entered the headquarters of ICU, he couldn't help walking in with a smile as big as the one he had had on his first day of Kindergarten twenty-three years ago. For him, it was more than just the end-of-year staff party. It was the first time he was going to see all his colleagues since his big promotion to senior operative.

As soon as he entered the building, several people immediately came up to congratulate him. It made him laugh a little – the fact that news travelled so fast in a top-secret place like the International Control Unit. Even though everyone knew not to spill the juice outside these walls, it was nearly impossible to keep a secret within them.

Markus Riley was now officially the youngest senior

operative in the agency. Originally his plan was to become a senior before turning thirty, but with the impressive track record Markus had, it didn't surprise many that he had achieved this goal two years earlier than planned.

"The only thing missing tonight is Cassandra," Markus mumbled whilst making his way to the make-shift bar in the conference room. Cassandra Young had been his partner for nearly two years now since ICU had recruited her a few years back in the United Kingdom. Cas was the first partner Markus could fully depend on. She was both mentally and physically one of the strongest people he had ever met. She had been hurt on a mission in Russia a couple of months ago, meaning he had to now face the ICU Christmas extravaganza by himself this year. In fact, that mission was the last either of them had been on. That mission helped him get his promotion early but had also landed his partner on an operating table for several hours.

Her ribs had been badly bruised, so bruised that one of her lungs had collapsed. Her leg had been crushed by a seventeen-ton forklift which broke her upper thigh bone. A human thigh bone is stronger than concrete and incredibly hard to break. Cas repeatedly joked that this was her sole achievement of the mission and that she had done something near-impossible. She figured that she deserved to be able to poke fun at her own condition after being horizontal for so many weeks – after all, hospital visitors don't entertain themselves.

As far as their bosses at ICU were concerned, the mission had been a success. They had accomplished what they were sent to Russia for but it certainly did not feel like a success to Markus. All he could think about for weeks after was the way she had screamed when that forklift crushed one of her legs. The screaming didn't last long as the pain had made her pass out in seconds, but the sound was burned in his memory. He remembered seeing her legs pointing in opposite directions, in a position so unnatural it almost made her look like a cartoon. Somehow it didn't seem fair to be celebrating the end of year and his promotion without her.

Markus could see Fred McMurchary, aka the big boss of ICU, make his way towards him through the cheerful crowd. The look he gave Markus clearly said *stay right there, I want to speak to you.* McMurchary was one of those people that often didn't have to say a word to make himself understood – the look and expressions on his face were enough.

"Good evening, Markus," said the large serious-looking man with a forced smile on his face. Smiling wasn't something McMurchary usually did. He had the ability to make even the most confident people feel jumpy and nervous. Markus couldn't help but think that the presence of his smile was less for congratulations and more because he needed something from him.

"Hello, sir. How are you?" He responded with a neutral but wary smile.

Of course, the gut feeling Markus had was correct. McMurchary ignored his question completely, "Once I've said a few words to welcome everyone, could you share some stories of your journey to becoming senior? Something inspirational and motivating for the younger generation." The words may have seemed like a request, but the tone of his voice clearly said otherwise. This was an order.

While McMurchary made his way to the stage, all Markus could think about was his unexpected speech. He would have to wing it, there was no time to prepare. *Why the hell didn't his boss tell him about this when he promoted him last week? What a douche. I'm supposed to be celebrating, not working.*

Markus was ordinarily one of the most confident agents in the field – he was used to handling himself in extremely unpredictable and high-pressured situations, situations that most people would never dream of finding themselves in – but he could feel himself becoming very nervous very quickly. Speaking in front of two hundred people had not exactly been part of his training to be an agent.

He got a fright when McMurchary announced his name, it was like waking up from a bad daydream, only to realise the daydream was about to come true anyway. The entire room turned to face him, applauding and cheering. He could see them cheer but all he could hear was the deafening thud of his own heartbeat. Suddenly he realised how absurd he was being. *You're being ridiculous. Stop being an idiot!* he berated himself as he made his way to the microphone.

"Thank you. Thank you all very much," he said with

only a slight tremble in his voice. He took a deep breath, blew out all his nerves and started his speech about his missions and victories – though likely in a different tone than McMurchary had expected.

"I would not be standing here tonight, talking about my journey to become a senior agent, were it not for my partner, Cas. As most of you know, I was promoted after finishing the SC5 mission in Russia. Well, the truth is that I would have never made it back without her. So, thank you, Cassandra, and I hope you're back soon. My thoughts are with you, partner. I owe you for next time." By now the nerves were starting to disappear, his voice no longer trembling and he continued to speak about his adventures with his usual confidence.

After telling the audience about four of his past missions, stories most of them already knew, McMurchary waltzed back onto the stage, body language practically shouting that Markus had spoken for long enough.

Markus yielded his spot as center of attention and thanked his audience again before making his way off the stage and towards the bar. On the way, he was met with his colleagues patting him on the shoulders and shaking his hand, a stream of 'well done's and 'good job's following him. Once he reached the back of the room, he heard the distinctive voice of Julia, speaking in a very different tone to all the others who had congratulated him. Julia was incredibly smiley and lovely to your face, but would stab you brutally in the back the second you turned around.

She was admittedly good at her job – *and not bad looking either*, Markus thought – …but she was a bitch you couldn't trust.

As he walked past the group of gossiping girls, he overheard Julia, "I can't believe he was singing her praises. I heard she fucked up that mission and nearly got them both killed!"

Sue joined in, saying, "If I were in charge, I'd get rid of her. She's a liability!" By the time Sue realised Markus was standing right behind her, able to hear everything she had just said, it was too late. Sue was one of the receptionists working for ICU Amsterdam, a twenty-something girly-girl who always came to work with a smile on her face. She was one of those people that was friends with everyone but people knew not to tell her any secrets as she loved a good gossip.

"Oh hi, Markus. Did you hear all that?" she said with an embarrassed look on her face. "I didn't mean that, about getting rid of Cas. I like her."

Markus knew exactly what Sue was like and decided to just ignore her. He couldn't help but make a snide comment to the Queen Bitch though, "I can't believe you still hold a grudge about Cas getting promoted before you, Julia. Jealousy is so unattractive," he said pointedly whilst walking away.

Markus decided to resign himself to work-related small talk with his work mates. A lot of the ICU staff could not help talking about work. This wasn't necessarily because they had nothing else to talk about, but was due to the fact that they couldn't talk about ICU related topics to other people. Even the people closest to them weren't allowed to know about ICU or what they did.

ICU or the International Control Unit was an organisation formed by a dozen countries over a decade ago, designed as a specialist unit to stop terrorism and corruption. The agency is still funded by those founding countries, but none of those governments have any say in the day to day running of the organisation. The ICU is intended as an independent body that operates in the interest of the world at large. Eleven years ago, leaders of those countries sat down and created the objectives, rules and regulations that ICU follows to curtail international threats to the safety and wellbeing of the populace. Possessing undercover assets in the most unimaginable places on earth, the ICU has been responsible for stopping terrorism and exposing corruption countless times, unbeknownst to ordinary people. Probably less than a handful of people in each country are aware of the ICU's existence. Even fewer are aware of its scope.

"Can I speak to you for a minute?" Danielle, Markus's former direct supervisor, said in a firm way that clearly suggested that it was about more than just celebratory holiday chat.

The short holiday break that everyone was looking forward to so much wouldn't last as long as planned for Markus. Danielle expected him at the office tomorrow at eight in the morning and the words she had used made it clear that the celebrations were over for Markus.

He was excited to start his first day as senior but he was also slightly disappointed that it had to be the day after the staff party. ICU's end-of-year parties had been a lot of fun the last couple of years. Once Danielle turned her back to Markus, he mumbled under his breath, "Fuck me, this better be worth it."

Before he could look away, she turned her head and fixed him with a pointed stare. "Excuse me?"

He had forgotten about her incredible hearing capabilities.

2

It was Saturday, 5:30 AM. Markus was wide awake with still half an hour to go before his alarm would make that godawful noise again. He normally never woke up before his alarm. The snooze button was usually his irresponsible best friend on days that he had stuff to do.

A quick egg and bacon fry-up seemed like the perfect plan now that he had so much time on his hands. Perfect plans don't always turn out that way, however. After a couple of bites, first day nerves started taking over and finishing his food was simply not an option anymore. Markus paced up and down his flat until he decided that he should probably just stick to his usual morning routine. Well, at least the routine he had before Cassandra, ICU, and the rest of the world had convinced him to start living a healthier lifestyle.

"Time for some coffee and a cigarette," he said to his

image in the mirror, in a manner that sounded like he had just found the solution to global warming.

After doing everything as slowly as possible, he still ended up at the office twenty-five minutes early. He had even taken the long route through the old centre of Amsterdam, but for some reason everything was going unusually smoothly today. Every traffic light turned green for him on the way. He laughed at the impossibility of it, since if the cards were turned and he was in a rush, every light would have conspired against him and turned red at his approach.

When Markus arrived at the office, it turned out he was not even the first there. McMurchary, Danielle and AJ were already in one of the meeting rooms, and by the look on their faces the atmosphere was not great. AJ was the manager of the Amsterdam branch and ran most operations in Europe from there. He was one of those people with whom you were never quite sure where you stood. He was mysterious, quiet and highly intelligent.

Markus entered the meeting room rather cautiously but as soon as he opened the glass door, the discussion the trio were having stopped. If these three weren't his bosses and the ones who had given him his promotion, he would have probably thought they were saying horrible things about him.

"Good morning, Markus," Danielle said with a comforting smile on her face. "Please have a seat."

As soon as he sat down, the argument continued. Markus just sat there.

McMurchary finished the heated discussion by saying, "Let's let Markus decide."

Markus had no clue what they had been talking about for the past five minutes. Since he had joined the table, the conversation had been so fast-paced that he had only been able to pick out certain words or phrases at the most. Trying to not sound too clueless, Markus answered with a strategic, "Well, I think I need a little more info before deciding on anything important."

"Right. Let me explain this to you as simply as possible. You are well aware that the newly appointed President of the United States was not our first choice. There is a chance that he might cause trouble for us. In the worst case scenario, he may very well start a war. Needless to say, this is not in anyone's best interest. AJ and I want to send you to Washington to infiltrate the White House so that we have eyes and ears on the inside. It would also mean that you are our back-up in case he does misbehave and we require someone to act fast. Danielle thinks it is too dangerous to put you in the lion's den, especially as it may end up being a long-term undercover mission. But we need someone we can trust."

Markus could tell by Danielle's face that she was about to explode. "Bollocks! Stop sugar-coating things, Fred!" She turned to Markus, "Yes, it might turn out to be a long-term undercover mission but if he does *misbehave* – as Fred calls it – and we need to take him out, you are going to be our secret weapon that will take care of the job. You will be ICU's kill switch to take out the President of the

United States. Fred is right that this may not be necessary, but if it is, it will be extremely dangerous and the chances of not getting out of there afterwards are high. Frankly, and meaning no disrespect, Markus, but there are other agents that are more qualified and have more experience with operations of this risk level."

"But we have chosen you for a reason," AJ cut in whilst giving Danielle a stern look. "We have been able to get our hands on the identity of someone who has completed the first training stage of becoming a secret service agent. Once you have passed the second stage, we can fix things so that you'll be assigned to the President's personal security detail. You were our first choice because of the resemblance between you and Jonathan Black."

Whilst handing Markus a photograph of Black, McMurchary took over the briefing, "If you accept the mission, we will need you to move to the States as soon as possible to become Jonathan Black and start the seventeen week training programme at the James J. Rowley Training Center in Washington, DC. As you know, agents usually do not get to choose their missions, but it seems like Danielle won't settle unless I give you a choice. So, it's up to you. What do you say?"

"It's an honour, Sir, I would love to take this on. Sorry, Danielle. I know you mean well but this could be a photograph of me. A photograph of me with a bad haircut and a tan, but a photograph of me. I don't see how anyone else could assimilate into the role as easily as I could."

"Great. That settles that. Your flight is in four hours."

McMurchary paused briefly to let that sink in, "I know this is probably a bit sooner than expected but we are on a tight schedule." He continued while sending a text, seemingly satisfied to move on to the next order of business, "Don't worry about your belongings. I've got people packing up your flat as we speak. AJ, can you brief Markus fully, please?"

"Sure. Come on, Markus. Let's head up to my office," he gestured for Markus to follow him. "I've got news that will make you a very happy agent, I think," AJ said whilst repeatedly pressing the elevator button like an impatient child.

AJ being so cheerful and chatty took Markus by surprise, he was usually quiet and straight to the point. He seemed like he was bursting to tell him something.

"Cassandra has been given the green light by the medical team. She'll be returning to work next week!"

"That's amazing news, AJ!"

"That's not all. Instead of coming back here on Wednesday, she'll be flying to Washington to join you, as your handler and go-to person."

"That's even better news! You weren't wrong, AJ. A happy agent indeed," Markus said, his smile broadening by the second.

"As we don't have a base in Washington, I thought I might as well send someone you know and trust along instead of one of our American operatives. I have arranged for you to be picked up by one of ours, Hannah Edelstein. She will collect you from the airport in Philadelphia and take you to your new house in DC. If there is anything you and Cas need, she will be your contact point over there. Just remember she has only been partially briefed about what you two are there for.

"I have put together a file for you which will tell you everything you need to know. There's also a background file on Jonathan Black in there. Use the time you've got during the flight to study and become him, in case you ever meet anyone that knows him. It's extremely important we get this right."

"Yes, sir. I understand."

3

After being fully briefed and prepped by AJ for a couple hours, it was time for Markus to make his way to the airport. He was flying to Philadelphia on a commercial flight departing from Schiphol.

Schiphol, one of the largest airports in Europe, was probably no more than a thirty-minute drive away from ICU's headquarters in Amsterdam, but because of its size it was essential to get there on time. The airport is so large that it can take longer to walk from the car park to your gate than to drive from the city centre to the car park.

On the way to the airport, Markus wasn't sure how to feel. Amsterdam had been his home base since he joined ICU years ago. Even though all his friends here were part of his cover and had no clue what he actually did, it was sort of a shame to leave so abruptly without any proper goodbyes.

However, when the car left the city, so too did his misgivings, making space for thoughts about his new job, his new home, his new life. He started daydreaming about what life would be like over there as an undercover agent working for the President of the United States. He'd heard stories and seen photos obviously, but he had never been quite so far from home before. The biggest unanswerable question he had was probably about the duration of the job – it could end up taking weeks, months, or perhaps even years. It bothered him, the fact that he would not find out when the sails would be homeward bound, or if he would even see his home again at all.

Of course, traffic was much busier now than in the morning when he had been able to race to ICU over the canal bridges and cobblestones with no bother. The traffic was so busy, Markus now had to rush through the crowded airport. Luckily, all of his belongings were being brought and checked in by someone else, meaning he was able to focus on getting to the gate as soon as he left the car.

Running from left to right through the busy hallways, Markus nearly ran over several people who clearly ignored or did not hear his desperate cries for them to watch out.

He made it. Just.

His face was covered in sweat and he was panting like he had just run a marathon, but he had made it. Markus was usually in pretty good shape and often went for runs longer than that run to the gate. He figured that he had the stress of starting a completely new life to blame for the excessive sweating. Maybe it was part of his new identity that he now was prone to sweating – something else to adjust to in his role as Jonathan Black. "Not a great start," he mumbled to himself while joining the back of the queue to board the plane. A mother carrying a small child in a baby sling gave him a comforting smile as if she knew that he needed something to make his day just a little bit better. Sometimes a smile, especially from a stranger can have a big impact. On this occasion it certainly did. As he smiled back at her and the child, he could feel the stress leave him. The expression on his face changed so quickly you would almost think that chemicals had to be involved, like the way morphine can make a smile appear even on someone in a lot of pain.

*

The plane was packed, mostly with families and couples going on holiday by the looks of it. He felt lucky once he got to his seat that it was an elderly couple sitting next to him – people who might make a little small talk but without any crying babies at least.

After two hours on the plane, Markus woke up from the noise the Brits in the row in front of him were making. It was clear that the pair had been doing some drinking since the plane had taken off, as their volume control seemed to be disappearing.

Time for a bathroom break, Markus thought when he saw that the elderly lady next to him was getting up. He hated the bathrooms on airplanes. They were way too small for someone as tall as him, especially when trying to sit down.

As Markus's knees were digging into the door, he discovered a napkin tucked oddly between the wall and the soap dispenser. He could see that it had something written on it. It was so stuck it partially ripped when Markus tried to pull it out. For a second, he considered just leaving the napkin where it was but then his curiosity took over and he pulled the soap dispenser away from the wall and wedged the napkin out. All it said in big red letters in what looked like crayon was:

HELP ME PLEAS. 13B

For a minute, Markus wasn't sure what to do as protocol for his mission told him to lay low during the transit. Minimal contact with civilians. "Only talk enough to remain inconspicuous," is what AJ had told him. "Don't draw attention to yourself."

He decided to check out the situation first before making any rash decisions. Seat 13B was in the opposite direction so he decided to take a stroll to the loos at the front of the cabin. Whilst walking to the front, he realised how lucky he was sitting next to the couple. The plane was like a daycare, children and babies on almost every second row. He shuddered to imagine a long-haul flight sat in the middle of it all.

Only two seats were occupied on the left side of row 13. The window seat was vacant, but the middle seat was taken by a young girl who Markus guessed was from somewhere in Eastern Europe. She looked about twelve. She was staring at the floor and as Markus attempted to catch her eye, the man next to her glared back at him sternly. He was middle-aged, had a massive beer belly, and was probably Russian judging by the look of his specific tattoos. Part of the Russian mafia, perhaps? No wonder the girl was too scared to look up, the man didn't look particularly friendly. In fact, he looked like the type of person you would definitely try to avoid when walking down a street at night.

Making a decision right now felt impossible. It suddenly felt as difficult to make a decision as it did when he was drunk and trying to choose the toppings on a pizza. Only this decision could affect a lot more than just his level of food satisfaction; it could affect his mission and potentially this young girl's life. In an ideal world, he would have swooped in to ensure the girl was safe, ready to physically defend her from the man if it proved necessary, but he knew this would compromise his cover. He made his way to the rear of the plane and found one of the cabin crew.

"Hi, excuse me. Could I speak to you in private for a moment? It's important," he said to the young steward who seemed to be in charge.

"Yes, of course. Follow me," the young man walked ahead of Markus to the little kitchen area at the back of the cabin. "What can I do for you, sir?" he said with a look of concern on his face. When a customer pulls you aside in this kind of industry, ninety percent of the time it's to complain about other passengers, or about issues that the staff have no control over.

Markus told the steward about the note he had found and pointed out the young terrified girl sat next to the man who had looked threateningly back at him. Satisfied that he was being taken seriously, Markus made his way back to his own seat. He felt bad having to wake the elderly couple, especially after overhearing the lady saying how she was a nervous flyer. He had no choice, however – the flight was full except for seat number 13A and he wasn't risking getting involved.

Despite handing over the situation, he still felt like he had to at least check up on the girl now and then. He leaned over to speak to the couple, "Excuse me, I am so sorry to disturb you but would you mind if we swapped seats so that I could take the aisle? I've had quite a lot of coffee today and I wouldn't want to keep waking you if I need to get up a few more times…" A little white lie, but luckily the couple didn't mind switching. They rearranged all their belongings and soon the lady fell back asleep.

The next five hours felt like an eternity. Markus went to the toilets at the front of the cabin at least every half hour, the passengers that were awake must have thought that he had the runs. The scene barely changed, the girl's gaze remained fixated on the floor. She could have been a wax sculpture in Madame Tussaud's, her movements were that minuscule.

*

Forty-five minutes to go and the girl in 13B was still staring at the floor while the man next to her was watching something on his tablet. Neither of the two had said a word to each other since Markus had first started checking up on them. Something was definitely off. According to the steward, the man and the girl had checked in together, which confirmed that they knew each other. But people that knew each other would likely at least say a few words every now and again. Markus was beginning to second-guess whether or not he should intervene himself.

As much as he tried to not get involved, he needed to be sure everything was in place for the girl to get any help she might need. He found the steward for an update on the situation and to find out what was being done. The steward tried to tell him that everything was under control, but when he realised that Markus was not going to take just that as an answer, he explained that he had spoken to the captain. The captain, in turn, had been in touch with authorities on the ground who had indeed found something strange with their documents. Police assistance had been requested upon arrival in Philadelphia.

Not even fifteen minutes later, the seatbelt sign lit up and the crew prepared the cabin for landing. The landing was incredibly smooth. Markus had never been on a plane this size before and he was expecting a bumpy ride from something so massive and heavy hitting the ground at that speed.

The crew asked all passengers to remain seated as per usual. Within minutes of landing, however, several policemen and special units were flooding the plane. Before most passengers realised anything was going on, they were taking the man and the girl from row 13 away with them. It all happened so quickly, the passengers at the back of the plane didn't notice anything at all. Whatever the police had discovered and whatever was to happen, Markus felt relieved that he had been able to help in some way. He was impressed. The police operation here had been smooth, quick and quiet.

4

The drive to his new home felt slightly awkward. Hannah Edelstein had been waiting for Markus in the arrivals hall like a proper chauffeur with a sign that read 'Jonathan Black' in big capital letters. At first he almost walked past her as the name didn't immediately ring a bell. Luckily she recognised him from the picture she had been given. Thanks to her wave and smile, the name on the cardboard sign suddenly made sense.

After a brief introduction, they made their way to the car park. She seemed to be in a rush. Markus could barely keep up now that he had a trolley full of his belongings to cart around. He figured that she had probably been waiting for some time while he had been trying to find his suitcases on the luggage belt. Whoever had packed up his apartment had managed to fit his whole life into four suitcases. He wondered how long it would take ICU to move another agent into his apartment. That apartment had been his home for the last six years. He hated the thought of someone else in his home, but then it dawned on him: he had no home anymore.

Once they got to the car Markus was at a bit of a loss. He wasn't sure how much he was allowed to share with Hannah so the best option seemed to be to continue in silence, at least for the time being. The silence felt tense. It didn't help that Hannah was walking ten steps ahead the entire route to the car. It made him feel like she could not wait to be rid of him.

The drive from Philadelphia to Washington DC was about three hours, as AJ had told him that morning. After driving in complete silence for 45 minutes, Markus felt the need to talk about something, anything was better than more of the awkward silence.

"So how long have you been with ICU?" It took Hannah a couple of moments to take in what Markus had asked. She had been deep in thought.

"Um, I've been with the agency for four years now – in the States since 2015 and in Canada before that. That's where they recruited me. I was a police officer before. What about you?"

"Eight years now, mostly in Europe. It's my first time in the States actually. I'm glad Jonathan Black doesn't need to have an American accent. I'm not sure how convincing I would be. I've never been very good with accents."

Markus had not been chosen purely because of his resemblance to Jonathan Black. Black was half-American and half-English, possessed the same athletic build and was only two years younger than Markus. They could have been brothers. Walking on this planet with so many people on it, it made one wonder how many doppelgangers we all could have without us knowing.

Jonathan Black had previously been a police officer in San Francisco but had recently been recruited to join the secret service. He had passed the first training stage in Georgia and was due to begin the second stage of training in a couple of weeks. Jonathan disappeared and the ICU took over his identity. What happened to the real Jonathan was something Markus would love to know but would probably never find out. The ICU had a way of making people disappear and it was an unwritten rule that you were not to ask too many questions. The only thing Markus had to do now was convince the few people who had met the real Jonathan during the interview process that he was one and the same. That, and pass the specialised seventeen-week training at the James J. Rowley Training Center in Washington DC. Piece of cake.

*

Markus was amazed by the stunning countryside they drove through to get to Washington. His mind was full of the stories his father had told him about America when he was a boy. His thoughts then naturally turned to memories of his father. He was deep in his past when Agent Edelstein broke into his reverie.

"What are you dreaming about?" Hannah asked. She had the strongest American accent he'd encountered.

"If I didn't know any better, I would think that you're American. You must have lived close to the border by the sounds of it. Where in Canada did you grow up?" Not wanting to dredge up more of the increasingly dark thoughts he was having about his father, he decided to avoid her question with one of his own. An obvious technique in changing the subject, maybe, but effective.

"I'm one-hundred percent Canadian, but yes, I lived near Niagara Falls until I was eleven and my family moved to Toronto after that. I studied in Toronto and joined the force there."

"Have you seen the house I'll be staying in?"

"I have. Actually, I'm the one who decorated and furnished the house, so I hope you like it."

"I'm sure I will. I'll be all right as long as it has a bed and a decent shower," Markus said with a smile on his face. At least this meant that the house he was going to be living in for the foreseeable future was clean and new. It would make a welcome change from some of the dumps ICU had made him and Cas stay in over the last few years.

"The house is near Brightwood and is about twenty-five minutes away from the White House. It's semi-detached, three bedrooms, two bathrooms, lounge and a separate dining area. It also has a very private sunny garden. As missions go, I expect you'll be pretty comfortable, at least at home. Your neighbour is a middle-aged pilot who works for Delta, so he only stays there a few times a week and will likely not cause you much hassle. I think that's pretty much all I can tell you just now. You'll figure out the rest when we get there," she said, glancing over to check his reaction.

"It sounds great – it sounds like a palace compared to the last place my partner and I stayed in. Thanks, Hannah." On their last mission, Markus and Cas were forced to hole up in a small room located underground that was part of the Russian sewage system. They had to sleep in an electricity cupboard and, while it was surprisingly not as dirty as you would expect, the smell was absolutely unbearable. Not quite the luxurious and high-flying life people think special agents must lead.

Now that the two of them had spoken at least a little bit, silence no longer felt as awkward. It was comfortable now, so comfortable Markus decided to rest his eyes for a while.

*

"Only one more hour if the traffic isn't too bad. You should open your eyes now. We're about to get into Baltimore, so there's lots to see for the next forty miles or so," Hannah said with a gentle voice, not wanting to wake him up too abruptly. Hannah knew too well that there was nothing worse than being woken up by loud voices when napping. The way Hannah's mother used to scream up the stairs in the morning had taught her to never wake up anyone that way. Whenever anyone asked Hannah about her parents, the way her mother always woke her up early even on days

33

she had no reason to was always one of the first things she thought of. Her mother always said sleeping was a waste of time. Maybe this was one teenage rebellion Hannah never fully grew out of: she loved sleeping. It was indisputably her favourite hobby, especially after she moved away from home – possibly made more enjoyable because of the feeling of defiance every time she took a nap.

"Oh…hey. Mmph. Sorry, I must have dozed off. Ha, I don't think I know anything about Baltimore except what's in the musical, Hairspray…"

Hannah laughed. "I'm not sure how accurate that is. Some parts of Baltimore can be a little sketchy. There's some nice architecture and the theatre district of town always promises a good night. My favourite part is the harbour, though. I remember sitting on a terrace for hours last summer just watching the boats come and go. Why don't we take a little detour through Baltimore harbour so you can tick that off your list?"

"Sounds great," Markus said while yawning and stretching his limbs as wide as he could in the small car.

After a quick drive via the harbour, they were soon back en route to Washington DC. His new home and life were so close now, the excitement and nerves were starting to build up again. The last hour of the drive Markus could not help himself but ask Hannah a million questions as his eyes darted left and right at the changing scenery out the window. There was so much to see and learn, he was starting to feel like a child on a road trip.

Although he had not actually left the car much in his

short time so far in the United States, he could tell that life here was going to be very different than his life had been for the past 10 years in the Netherlands. Everything was bigger here, just like his father had told him. He remembered how animated his father would get when describing the enormous portions of food you would find in America. He chuckled a little when he thought about the terrible jokes his father would make about that. Judging by the people he could see walking around, for once his father had spoken the truth. Hannah gave him a questioning look but didn't ask.

"This is it, Markus. Somerset Place. Your house is the white one with the porch over there on the left."

It looked like an interesting neighbourhood with beautiful detached villas on one side of the street, though there were buildings that looked like council houses to Markus further down the road. It felt strange being on this side of the divide.

Markus walked up the path to the house he was told was now his. He fit the key in the lock and opened the door.

"Here we go."

5

Markus spent some days settling into the new house and getting to know the neighbourhood. It was now Wednesday. It was the day Cassandra was due to join him. Her flight wasn't expected for another three hours, but Markus was already waiting. He had been waiting impatiently for this day for what felt like an eternity.

He was so excited to see her, it made him feel nervous. Cassandra was his best friend and, to tell the truth, his only real friend these days. They always had so much fun together that it certainly felt like they were more than just work partners. If he was being honest with himself, Markus had often wished they were more than even just friends, but he knew that relationships between ICU partners were not allowed unless it was part of the cover story. There had always been a little harmless flirtation between them though, so acting like they were a couple would be easy.

Depending on the length of this mission, going back to being strictly colleagues would likely be the more difficult act to put on, at least to Markus. He was looking forward to having Cas as his girlfriend, even if it was just pretend. He was unsure how she felt about it.

Unlike the day he had left Amsterdam, today was one of those days where everything moved slower than he wished. He tried to watch some TV to kill some time, but even the worst Jerry Springer screaming match couldn't distract him from the feelings of impatience and overexcitement that were currently making him pace up and down the living room.

Something more active was necessary to stop him from wearing a hole into the carpet. He decided to take a stroll to the local shops he had discovered the other day to buy Cas a little welcome to the USA present.

*

Buying presents for other people was probably not one of Markus's strongest skills. He visited several small gift shops but was having no luck – everything felt too impersonal. He decided to go back to the bookshop he had visited two days ago. Nothing could beat a good book to help relax Cas and help her settle in.

Markus loved spending time in bookshops, especially second-hand ones. The smell of pre-loved books was like a drug to him. He could spend hours nosing through the shelves, imagining others before him curling up and getting lost in the stories hidden between those well-worn pages.

"Jonathan! It was Jonathan, wasn't it?" The elderly man spoke when he saw him enter the shop.

"I'm impressed you remember. Not many would remember a customer's name after just one visit," he said as he reached over the counter to shake the man's hand. During Markus's last visit, the two men had spent over an hour talking about their favourite books and about the city. He was the first person Markus had made a connection with since Hannah had dropped him off, which was why their small talk had progressed to a proper discussion.

"I only remember the nice ones," said the owner with a cheeky smile on his face. Freddy's name was easy to remember as the shop was called 'Freddy's Book World'. Freddy was a short stocky man with round Harry Potter-style glasses that made him look like he was squinting at everything. He was important in the neighbourhood. Freddy was the person that passed on news between the residents of the community, he was the person that made what was an area of a big city feel more like a small town. That day he had been speaking to Freddy, Markus could not help but notice how many people would pop into the bookshop or wave from outside, and Markus could see why. Even though it was only the second time he had met Freddy, he was already very fond of him. Usually, it took Markus a lot longer to warm to strangers. His trust in mankind was minimal, perhaps because of all the horrible things he had witnessed over the last several years while working for the agency.

"I'm feeling a little lost here. Maybe you can help me, Freddy. I'm looking for a book for my girlfriend. I know she's into her sci-fi and I've definitely seen a romance novel or two lying around that she always pretends isn't hers. Neither of those are really my cup of tea. Could you help me find something decent?"

"Of course, that's what I'm here for, after all. Give me a minute and I'll have a look for you, son."

*

After finding a book he thought she'd like, it was time to get back to the house to pick up the car. It was perhaps still slightly early to leave and he would likely have to wait around the airport for a while, but under no circumstances was he going to be late to pick up Cassandra.

Good thing that airports had always fascinated Markus. He often tried to imagine what was going on behind the scenes when sitting around waiting for a flight. There was o many people moving and working on a dozen separate things simultaneously – all cogs in a massively complex machine. The meticulously precise logistics it required amazed him.

The traffic on the way to the airport was busy. It was fortunate that he left so early. As Markus followed the exit towards the airport, he still had half an hour until her plane was expected to land. Luckily it was a lovely day and the airport had a manmade lake where people could take a stroll whilst watching the planes come and go. Markus was beginning to feel nervous again, a feeling that had become all too familiar recently. If he hadn't had good reason to feel nervous in the stress of moving half-way across the world about to embark on a crucial and difficult mission, he would have diagnosed himself with anxiety. He wondered whether feeling this way had anything to do with getting older – years ago, none of this would have made him the least bit concerned. Not Markus. He was known for being coolheaded and rational. That was what made him perfect for his chosen career. It was crucial as an agent that you were able to deal with any situation calmly. He did not like that these feelings of nervousness seemed to be becoming more frequent. It made him doubt his capabilities, his skills, himself. Doubt was what got you killed in the field.

The agency had decided it was best for Cassandra to take on a different identity as well. Jonathan Black was picking up Natasha Connelly, his girlfriend. He was just thinking that it would definitely take some time to get used to the names when he suddenly heard a familiar voice. "Jonathan, over here. Surely you wouldn't mind carrying the bags of the woman you love?" she said cheekily as she threw her arms around his neck.

This was so typical of Cassandra: playing the role with a hundred percent believability but taking the piss out of it all at the same time. Of course, no one but Markus would ever know that her little performance was meant to ridicule their new identities.

As soon as he felt her warm arms around his neck, all the feelings he hadn't felt for weeks came rushing back. For a second, he felt paralyzed. He had secretly had a crush on Cassandra since the day she had joined the agency. To Markus, she was the perfect woman: sexy, smart, incredibly determined and funny – often in an intelligent, cheeky way that Markus loved.

"It's so good to see you! How was your flight?"

"All right. It would have been a lot better if the man next to me had brushed his teeth before getting on the plane," she scrunched up her face in distaste. "So how is Washington? You settled in yet? I was here once for a cheerleading competition when I was eleven, not that I remember much apart from the fact that we lost."

"A cheerleader, you? I'll file that away as blackmail material. No surprise you only remember losing, you're still a terrible loser," he ribbed her and attempted to avoid the fist she half-heartedly aimed at his chest.

"A terrible loser? Me? What would make you think that? Oh, and also, please never call me Natasha. Let's go for Tash. They could not have picked a more sickening name. Nataaaaaasha – ugh, I hate it!"

"Come on, I'll take you for a spin in my new ride," Markus said in his best American accent – which sounded about as convincing as Leonardo DiCaprio's South African accent in Blood Diamond.

The drive back to their new home was like an amateur

41

comedy show, a very long comedy show as the traffic was barely moving for two hours. It was almost worth recording. This is what he had missed most about Cassandra: her amazing sense of humour. The banter between the two of them sometimes seemed endless, especially after not seeing each other for an extended amount of time. Even discussing their assignment made their long, dangerous task ahead became enjoyable.

"Ten minutes, then we're home, Natasha," Markus said with a chuckle. She should have expected him to make it a point to use her new name after she told him not to.

"I'm going to ignore that one. So, what's our house like?"

"It's American, very American, but in a good way. Massive rooms, big open-plan kitchen with an American double-door fridge of course. If we were children, it'd be the perfect place to play hide-and-seek. The living room has exquisite French doors leading to a private garden. Shops are in walking distance to the property," his voice jokingly took on the tone of an estate agent as he described their new home. "Seriously though, this place is down-right palatial compared to some of the shitholes the agency has put us in before."

"Thank God. I was scared it would be like Russia all over again. This sounds almost like a holiday, shame you'll be working all the time…" she would have sounded sincere had it not been for the cheeky grin on her face. Her expression soured, "I'm not sure how I feel about this stay-at-home girlfriend role. I was obviously excited when

I got the green light from the medical team, but I had sort of hoped for a little more action for my comeback. I think I might need to find some new hobbies to stop myself going insane from boredom."

"You could try learning to cook a little so we don't end up with food poisoning again," Markus said, trying not to laugh too much. The last time she had cooked for him was over a year ago in Istanbul. Neither of their stomachs had been able to handle the 'chicken soup' she had made, seeing as how probably eighty percent of the chicken had been raw. Markus had never trusted her cooking again. He also still could not face chicken soup.

6

"Markus, I've got news about your training," Cas shouted up the stairs. "Get up. You're starting in less than two weeks."

After a few minutes without a response, Cas decided she would have to get him up herself. When she opened the door to his room, she realised why he had chosen it: this room had heavy-duty curtains that blocked out all the light. Hers were so flimsy and sheer, she'd naturally woken up with the rising sun. "Get up lazy bones," she shouted, smacking him with one of the pillows. "I thought you were being a gentleman when you offered to give me the room with the en suite, but you just wanted this one for the curtains, didn't you?"

"This isn't the way a girlfriend wakes up her boyfriend," he said, smiling with a sleepy voice. He yawned and stretched exaggeratedly, rolling around in the king-sized bed. That earned him another smack with the pillow right in the face. By now Markus was awake enough to respond. He pulled her on to the bed and ripped the pillow out of her hand.

The pair ended up in a position they hadn't been in before – at least not in this situation and not in a bed. She was lying on top of him, their faces were only inches apart. He could feel her breath gently brushing past the side of his face.

Of course they had been very close to each other before during missions, often sharing cramped living spaces. But this felt different. She was staring right into his eyes, looking at him in a way that was new to him. Neither of them said a word.

For a moment, he considered moving her off of him. Instead, he did the unthinkable. He pressed his lips against hers. He had fantasised about this for the past two years.

Their eyes closed.

She kissed him back.

It felt amazing and wrong all at the same time. They were partners – they weren't supposed to be anything more than that. Any relationship between them was only supposed to be part of their cover for this mission.

"I don't know if we should do this," he reluctantly said, though still playfully biting her lip.

"I don't care about what we should or shouldn't do. We're a million miles away from home. Also, I'm your handler, so I make the rules." Her tone said that she was in charge and that she wanted this. She was the one initiating things now and it took him by surprise.

They had gone this far, there was no turning back, he thought to himself. Plus, she had made a valid point: they were so far away from home with no interfering eye of ICU watching them, they made the rules now. He decided to move her off him, but with a different intention than before. He flipped them over, his weight on her body, and kissed her all over. He started at the side of her neck. Then he tenderly nipped at her earlobe. The way her body was pushing back against his told him he was doing something right.

He put his right hand under her top, slowly sliding up and moving between her skin and the bottom of her bra. He lowered his head and started biting and sucking one of her breasts through the fabric of her top and bra while he massaged the other with his hand. He switched and made sure both sides got the same level of attention.

"I think you should take this off," he said with a husky voice. He was done with tasting fabric – he wanted to taste her.

Before he even finished speaking, she had unclipped her bra with one hand, allowing him access to her nipples. He started gently rolling her nipple between his thumb and index finger, softly squeezing it, while still kissing her neck and lips all the while.

She rolled over to sit up and take off her top and bra fully. He leaned forward to kiss her, but she made it clear that she was in charge by pushing him forcefully back down on to the bed – he had had his fun exploring her body, now it was her turn.

"Just relax. You can play with these later…" she said while she began to massage his arms. She moved slowly, sensuously kneading one, then the other, before moving on to his chest and then his legs. Working her way up his legs, she made sure she went just a little bit higher each time, her touch gentle and teasing. He was rock hard. She hadn't even touched him there yet.

The contour of his member in his tight boxers did not disappoint her. She kissed it through the fabric the way he had kissed her breasts. He moaned as soon as her lips put on a little pressure. His nipples were next – she bit and kissed them one at a time. She could feel him press his crotch against her body, eliciting a small involuntary groan from her as he rubbed against her.

Markus was done with this teasing massage. He wanted to go further, to see and taste all of her. "Lie on your back," he demanded. The look in his eyes made her give in. She did what he asked. He pulled off the rest of her clothes in one swift movement and finally, she was naked, the woman he had fantasized about so much. She was beautiful.

He was done with this gentle foreplay. He was ready to get rough and dirty. He pushed her legs apart and lowered his lips on to her stomach. Kiss by kiss he worked his way down, her legs tensing as he did. She let out a loud moan as his mouth closed over her.

She tasted better than anything or anyone he had

ever had before. She exceeded all the expectations his fantasies had given him. When he looked up, he could see her fingers digging into the mattress. Her eyes were shut. She was on another planet.

She sighed, exhausted and spent from the strength of the pleasure she had just felt. She moved to return the favour but he stopped her. "Next time," he said with a look that told her what he wanted. He started off gentle and slow, rubbing his erection against her inner leg. She moaned when he finally entered her. She needed a minute – luckily he knew instinctively without her having to say anything. He lay on top of her, kissed her. Once she was used to him, the animal inside of him came out. They acted as if neither of them had had sex in years. Or maybe it was the years of pent-up longing for each other that now brought out this intensity between them.

Sweat was dripping down his face. She was close. He had her nails in his back. She tried to hold off to prolong the pleasure but she no longer had any control. She screamed.

Her body tensed around him. It was all he needed. As she writhed in pleasure, he groaned and came inside of her.

*

They lay there for a long time after, collapsed and exhausted. Neither of them moved except for their heavy breathing, as they both thought about what had just happened.

"Do you think we made a mistake?" she asked while rolling over to lie beside him.

"I don't care if it was a mistake. If it was, it was one of the best mistakes of my life," he said, smiling at her. "At least no one can say that we don't take our cover story seriously," he said laughing and turning to give her a kiss.

"I'd be lying if I said I hadn't thought about that happening before," she said somewhat embarrassedly before pulling the duvet over her head.

The two of them lay there for a while longer in silence. Reluctantly, she knew it was time to get on with what she had come upstairs for in the first place. The afterglow was gone and it was time to get on with their mission.

"We need to go to a hairdresser soon to make you look more like the real Jonathan. I've done some digging and we'll need to go shopping as well because your wardrobe doesn't really fit Jonathan Black's style," she said, the change in her demeanour almost jarring. "You start part two of the training here in Washington in thirteen days. We'll need to take you through the first part Jonathan already finished in Glynco in Georgia before that. I've booked us flights to go that way tomorrow morning. We'll stay there for four days and then we're flying to San Francisco for a week. That leaves us two more days here, then you'll start the seventeen week training." She paused and tried to soften the mood, "Seventeen weeks is a long time. I'll try to learn to feed you without killing you in that time." She smiled but Markus could tell it wasn't quite genuine.

"Sounds good." That was the only thing Markus was able to say. He knew how she felt about her role during this mission, but there was nothing he could say that would change that. He felt terrible about having to leave her alone during the seventeen week training, especially leaving her alone to play the dutiful waiting girlfriend. That wasn't her at all. Despite how often she claimed to dislike the human race during their missions, she was someone who loved being around people. Markus knew that she only said those things because of some of the evil bastards they had dealt with since working for ICU – the awful things they had seen could put anyone off humanity. Sometimes it was hard to know the difference between the good and the bad ones, though.

Cas struggled with the thought that the only person here she trusted was good was leaving her alone for three months. She would have to try to find something or someone else to keep her from becoming a hermit.

7

They were waiting to get off the plane at Brunswick Golden Isle Airport near Glynco in Georgia. Natasha was chatting to the lady next to her about what there was to do in the area, all the while holding Jonathan's hand. Out in public, Cas would play the perfect girlfriend: hold his hand, act sweetly and playful with him. But as soon as no one was watching, the act disappeared.

Markus was confused. It made him wonder how she really felt about them sleeping together. Did she regret it? Neither of them had spoken about it since they had left the bed that one morning. He thought about talking about it. He wanted to bring it up but he was not sure how. Something inside him feared that she would tell him it had been a one-time slip-up. After spending that day together preparing for this trip, they had both gone to bed. Their own beds. At the break of dawn the next morning, alarms had gone off, and their routine had been the same as it had been previously. Markus had struggled to get up and Cassandra was her usual energetic self. They both acted like nothing had happened.

Glynn Plaza Shopping Center was the first stop on their list after picking up their rental. The car, an old Suzuki truck, looked like it had been rented by at least a dozen terrible drivers. The amount of bumps and scratches made it look like it was near its end. The only thing new about it was the new car smell air freshener someone had hung from the rear-view mirror. It almost made it seem like they were driving their actually new Cherokee back in Washington. Almost.

Before checking out the training area and all the places the real Jonathan had been to during his training here, they had to buy some clothes that fit with Markus's new hairstyle. The plan was to make him look as much like Jonathan Black as possible in case they met anyone who had met him. Markus was nervous at that thought, he couldn't wait for the next couple of weeks to be over. Once the first week or two of training was done, he should have established himself enough by then that playing this role would be a lot more comfortable. The real Jonathan had lived in the US for ten years, which meant that Markus had to learn some American slang. Luckily, both Markus and Jonathan had spent considerable time in the United Kingdom, so their accents did not sound too different. All he had to do was to turn his European tones into more of an American twang.

Cas couldn't help teasing him a little as they entered the shopping centre. "I don't understand why you don't like your new hairstyle. It's so 90's. You're one of the cool kids now," she said laughing whilst giving his bum a little squeeze.

His hair looked as though someone had put a plant pot on top of his head before cutting it.

"Natasha, you're so funny. Have I ever told you that, Natasha?" Needling her about her much-hated name was the only rebuttal he had at the moment.

"Have a look at these," Cas said as she handed Markus her phone. She had made a folder of pictures she had found on Jonathan's social media.

"Why do I have such terrible style? First this haircut, now I have to look like a complete dork. I can't believe how unattractive having bad taste can make me look." He sighed. He used to think that undercover missions were cool. The stories he heard from other agents had made them sound like James Bond-themed holidays. No one had warned him about this. No one told him about the potential risk of ending up with the worst possible haircut and outfit imaginable. No wonder Cassandra hadn't brought up what happened between them. After all, his sex appeal had been destroyed, a bit more gone with each snip of the scissors.

"Well, luckily no one has to find you attractive since Jonathan has already scored a hottie," she said pointing both her thumbs at herself with a wink. It made him smile, but he was still confused inside whenever she started being flirty with him. If only Cassandra were more transparent.

She was right, though. He was here on a mission, not to attract lots of women. It made him feel young – he hadn't worried this much about someone liking him since he was a teenager. He was a bit frustrated with himself and the stupidity of his thoughts. It was her fault, he decided. Her acting was too good. As soon as she took on the role of his girlfriend, he felt warm, loved and special. Moments later, she would be his mission partner again and the feeling would disappear. He never used to have problems switching between roles moment to moment. Something had changed in his head after they had slept together.

After spending a good hour laughing and making jokes about potential outfits, they had found a couple of things to fit his new style. It was the first time either of them had spent time in an American mall. Everything was bigger than back home – even boxes of cereal were available in sizes about three times bigger. There was so much to do, they decided to have lunch near the shopping centre and do some more damage to the ICU accounts after. One of the perks of working for ICU: unlimited shopping allowances. They were allowed to buy anything under ten-thousand euros.

"How do you feel about this? It's just around the corner," Cas said, shoving her phone in his face. She had it so close he had to push it away ten inches to actually see anything.

"Proper American food. Looks good to me. I'll get the car if you wait here with all my beautiful new clothes. Don't worry if you lose any, ha."

"This is nice," he remarked once they were seated on the little white chairs at the restaurant. "Is it just me, though, or has that guy over there been staring angrily at us ever since we walked in?" It was one of those things they had learned during their ICU training: always scan everyone around whenever you enter a room. It became such a habit, agents usually do it even when not on an active mission.

"It does sort of feel like maybe he knows you."

"He doesn't look like the kind of person that would be at the Federal Law Enforcement Training Center to me. I guess you shouldn't judge a book by its cover but, to me, it looks like he might work at the local hairdressers or a beauty salon."

"Ha! Maybe he's just horrified at your hairstyle." She quickly sobered, "Hmm. He certainly isn't hiding the fact that he's looking at us. Okay, plan: I'll go to the bathroom. Then we'll know whether he's looking at you or at me."

Cas got up and made her way to the toilets. The man's eyes followed her for a moment, but then they were back on Markus. As soon as Cas was out of sight he got up and made his way over to the table.

"Oh no, here we go," Markus mumbled.

"Oh no! Here we go!" Apparently, Markus had mumbled too loudly as the man mocked him with his own words. "Really, that's all you've got to say after being in my bed several dozen times? You said I was more than just a fuck. You said that you would call. That was five weeks ago, asshole. You could have just said that all you wanted was sex instead of telling me you were falling in love." The man finished speaking and stood there, clearly waiting for a response but Markus was stunned. He had no idea what to say.

Markus was usually fast and sharp responding to people. He was a quick-thinker – it made him good at his job. This was certainly a first. He was at a complete loss as to what to say to this man accusing him of leading him on for what sounded like weeks. A man as camp as Christmas. The brief on Jonathan Black had not prepared him for this.

After not getting the response he was hoping for – or any response at all – the man continued, "Is that what you do? String people along, fucking them for weeks while telling them sweet little lies?"

"Sorry, what?" Cassandra reappeared. "I'm Natasha, Jonathan's *wife*. Please repeat what you just said."

This put the man into almost a big a state of shock as Markus was in, but only for a moment. "You're married? To a woman. Honey, you're married to a greedy bastard – having it both ways. And you, you're a dirty douchebag," he punctuated the last with his finger stabbing into Markus's chest. He spun around and walked away. He certainly knew how to make an exit. The host looked visibly relieved the glass door didn't shatter as the man slammed it as hard as he could on his way out. One more middle finger as he walked past the window, and then it was Cassandra's turn for dramatics.

With a twinkle in her eye that only Markus could see,

Cas then stormed out of the restaurant like a woman who had just found out she had been cheated on. Actual tears streamed down her face – her acting skills were unbelievable.

This left Markus standing there, with the customers who had witnessed what had just happened looking at him in disbelief and disgust. Markus felt mortified. He threw a twenty on the table for the drinks they had ordered but had never had and tried to make his escape. The number of angry looks was astonishing. Apparently everyone in the restaurant had been watching their real life soap opera.

Once outside, Markus jumped in the passenger seat and they drove off in silence. They remained silent long enough to make sure no one who just witnessed the whole kerfuffle would see. Then the laughter started.

"How the hell did no one find out Jonathan is into men when they were doing background checks?" Markus was laughing so hard, Cas could barely make out what he was saying. Both of them were astonished that ICU could have missed something so important. Jonathan Black was a closeted gay. So deep in the closet he was probably somewhere in Narnia.

"He kept that secret very well," Cas said once they had calmed down a bit. "I checked all his social media, all his messages, his mail. Nothing even suggested he was interested in men."

"Well, at least that means I can keep you as my hot girlfriend," he said, giving her a cheeky wink.

The plan had originally been to do more shopping after

lunch but since lunch had hilariously been cut short, they decided to just get a quick takeaway and do more research. More research was clearly needed.

"Can you grab me a cheese and chorizo panini? I'm scared to go in there in case I run into more of my sexual past. I knew meeting someone the real Jonathan had met before was going to be awkward, but I didn't expect it to be that bad. Make it two paninis."

"Hubby, you *are* a greedy bastard," she said before closing the car door on him. He couldn't help but start laughing again.

8

Exhausted from the excitement of the day, Markus dropped on to the bed as soon as he got in to the hotel room. They had spent the rest of the afternoon driving around the training area, checking out several places Jonathan had probably been to. They had talked about the real Jonathan and about what Markus could expect once he started his training in Washington, DC. Cassandra was clearly taking her job as his handler very seriously. She had done her homework and found out loads about the training ahead. She had tons of useful information, but for some reason she had been very matter-of-fact since she had got them lunch. She was telling him what he needed to know, but without voicing her own opinion about anything. If he didn't know her better he would have thought that she had used up all her laughs after the incident in the restaurant. She had barely smiled since.

They had rented one room with a double bed. He hoped that staying in such close proximity of one another all night long would trigger some sort of talk about what had happened between them. At the least, he'd like to know why she was suddenly acting so strangely. It surprised him how they had managed to talk all afternoon without really saying anything. The way they talked was different – it was usually more fun and personal. In the past, they had often spoken about their childhoods and lives before ICU, how they felt about certain things or people, things good friends would talk about. He wondered what had changed since their stop at the panini shop. The jokes, mostly ones ridiculing his new style, had been endless while they were shopping. After she was gone ten minutes in the shop, he could no longer get her to laugh even at Jonathan's secret love life.

"Do you fancy watching some TV?" he asked, quickly adding, "Or maybe listening to some music?" He hoped she would pick the latter as that made talking more likely. Luckily for him she wasn't fussed. He put on some chilled background tracks, setting the perfect mood to really talk.

As she got ready for bed in the bathroom, he planned out the way he was going to start a serious conversation with her. But of course things did not go as planned.

As soon as she opened the bathroom door, all his thoughts vanished. He couldn't help getting excited like a teenage boy when she came walking towards him, only in her pyjama shorts and tank top. Her long brown locks spilled over her shoulders, covering her nipples which would have otherwise shown through the thin white fabric. She was gorgeous and he was certain that he didn't want the other morning to be a one-time thing. Not only was she stunning, he felt a connection with her he had never felt with anyone else before. He started to feel like he might be falling in love. Even the thought of that possibility startled him. Markus had always struggled with the thought of being in love. How and when do you know? Is the feeling different for everyone? All these questions ran through his head as he got a funny, warm feeling in his stomach.

Cas got into the bed, covering herself with the duvet up to her chin and looked at him with a soft, sweet smile. All he could do was give her a warm smile back. They lay like that for a while just looking at each other in silence until the moment was broken by the noise of her phone vibrating on the hard nightstand surface.

"It's AJ apologising for the slip-up in Jonathan's background check."

Neither of them really minded as it gave them some decent laugh material for the next couple of days – at least, if Cassandra's ability to laugh would return. She messaged AJ back anyway as she was required to pass on any relevant information and check in to the manager in charge of the operation at head office. It was part of her role as Markus's handler.

After she put her phone away, she turned to face him, "Markus, I don't like this assignment. I wish we could go back." Her sweet smile had disappeared, making space for a different look, one that Markus had not seen before. She looked sad.

"What makes you say that? I thought you would like spending all this time exploring the States. And you get to do it with me?" he said half-jokingly but really hoping she would agree.

"I do like that. That isn't the problem. I have a feeling that this mission is not going to end well. Whatever way I play this forward in my head, it doesn't end positively for us. If the President doesn't do anything tragically wrong, we might end up being undercover for the next three years, or seven if he gets re-elected. That's a long time to just be someone's girlfriend. But being here for three years without any problems is the best possible scenario. What if you get ordered to kill him? Even if you manage to escape alive, you'll be the world's most hunted terrorist. It won't be like other missions where the ICU tech team can remove any evidence or video footage and blame someone else. This is the President of the United States, the most powerful man in the world depending on who you ask. Our careers would be over and we'll be spending the rest of our lives in hiding. I know that most of our missions have the risk of one or both of us ending up dead, but this feels different...I guess I'm just scared," she said quietly.

Markus had been hoping for a heartfelt chat tonight but this was not quite what he had planned. This was so unexpected that he didn't know what to do or say except take Cassandra's hand and give her a comforting squeeze.

All day long he had thought that she was acting strangely because of the other morning. He was so wrong. How unprepared they had been running into one of Jonathan's past lovers so unexpectedly had made her think about all the dangers of this mission. Yesterday had not been on her mind at all. He was relieved and shocked at the same time. Cassandra was one of the most dedicated and fearless agents he knew – this was not like her at all. Usually she was the one that would always put in one hundred percent whenever they got a new assignment. It was in her nature to be driven and focused.

She knew that he was lost for words but that was okay for now. She felt relieved now that she had said what had been on her mind since getting off the plane.

"I get what you're saying, Cas, and I've thought about some of it myself but I don't think we have much of a choice at this point. Going rogue and running away is not an option. Being on ICU's most wanted list is definitely worse. The thought of being in the same undercover position for three years is killing me too. I know you're right, though. It probably is the best way this could turn out. I think we need to just take it day by day and make the most of life here. You could do or learn some amazing things in three years. You might end up becoming the next Beethoven," he said while giving her a hopeful smile.

"Thank you."

Finally he felt brave enough to make a move – only not with the same intentions as before their talk.

Tonight was not a night where sex was on the menu. He put his arms around her like a real boyfriend would and cuddled her until they both fell asleep.

*

"Time to get up, mister. I've booked us a dolphin and whale boat trip this morning," Cassandra said with a big smile on her face. Something inside her had changed since their chat. She seemed to be back to being her energetic, happy self. This was because she knew that Markus was right. She had decided to do exactly what he had told her and take things day by day. Her plan was to treat the whole mission like a long holiday, one that would hopefully end as well as most holidays. She was excited to tell him about all the things she would do whilst he was at the training centre. Cooking classes, fitness and art were some of the things on her to-do list. She probably talked for twenty minutes straight telling him about all the things she had already researched since waking up a couple hours ago. Markus usually hated the way she was in the morning: too happy, too energetic and way too loud but he was able to appreciate it today. Being able to help her feel good and make her smile made him feel good about himself. There was a brief moment where he considered that maybe her new-found happiness wasn't real, but this was only because he knew how good Cassandra was at putting on a show. Being able to make anyone believe whatever she wanted was probably her greatest talent. She didn't need to take lessons for that one.

"It's going to be great. Can we agree to not have any work chat today? We can just be a regular couple enjoying each other's company, the dolphins and Brunswick."

"Sure," Markus gave her a nod. Things could not be better, especially compared to the odd day they had before. It was a warm, sunny day for this time of year and he was going to spend all day with Cas as a regular couple. He felt relieved. She seemed genuinely happy.

The boat trip departed from Brunswick, the second-largest urban area on the Georgia coast. The city itself had lots to offer in terms of tourism and American history, one of Markus's favourite subjects. The Lover's Oak Tree was on their list of things to visit after the tour, one of the area's most popular attractions because of its size and age. Said to date back to the 12th century and one of the biggest trees in the world, it often features in wedding photos or art projects. Cas had a thing for trees. She claimed that she loved listening to them – that the sound of a white birch in the wind was like music to her ears, especially at night when everything else was silent. She believed that every tree had its own melody and that the strength of the wind determined what song it would play for you.

It was a day neither of them would forget anytime soon. They had been on so many exciting adventures together that a day as normal as this was memorable. All they had done throughout the day was normal touristy stuff. It really felt like they were ordinary people on holiday.

The next few days were so nice, neither of them felt like moving on to San Francisco. Chances were a lot higher that people would recognize Jonathan over there. They would have to be more cautious and the relaxed holiday they were currently having would likely have to end.

9

There were only two more days before Markus started at the James J. Rowley Training Center. They had spent a lot of time preparing for the training over the past week in San Francisco. Thankfully the trip there had been flawless with no dramatic incidents in any restaurants or public places. Cas had forced Markus to wear shades and a cap every step of the way just in case more ghosts from Jonathan's past appeared. Luckily that wasn't an unusual look in San Fran. They could not afford to draw any more attention this early on in their mission. Even though they both found the situation in Glynco hilarious, they knew it had put their mission at risk. Any unnecessary attention could blow their cover.

Most of the training was very similar to the training Markus had received when he was first starting out at ICU. At this stage, the main skills he would be taught were physical: protection techniques, emergency first-aid, firearms, endurance and control tactics – all things he had done before. He assumed that this part was going to be easy for him. For someone who spent such little time working out, he was incredibly fit. When he had been younger, people would often ask how often he went to the gym, and he would proudly tell them that he had never even been to one. It was only when he started working for ICU that he began to work out to become stronger and faster. For the first two or three years, he was a regular at the gym underneath the office in Amsterdam. Since then, the urge to work out had become more sporadic. Still, Markus knew that the hardest parts for him would be computer-related or desk-bound work. Sitting still for long periods of time was not his strong suit. On top of that, the secret service systems were probably completely different to the ones at ICU. The real Jonathan Black would have had the advantage of working with the American police system for years, assuming that there were more parallels there than with ICU's systems.

*

The thought of spending seventeen weeks without Markus was making Cassandra feel lonely. Even though he was still around, she already felt it like an invisible blanket weighing her down. It made everything she did require more effort and it was exhausting. When she realised she was already letting these negative thoughts influence her this much, she knew she would need to find things to keep herself busy or else she would just end up being miserable.

She was at least going to try. She was going to try to make the most of her life whilst she was here. She had to keep on reminding herself to see all this as something positive. It was just a long holiday during which she would learn and discover loads of new skills. As she repeated these thoughts, she began to believe it but as soon as she stopped consciously trying to believe it, the heaviness would creep back.

The last day with Markus was going to be hard. She knew she would be okay once he was actually gone, but the build up to the moment felt like a lot to deal with. She decided not to let Markus in on the way she was feeling. Not just now. He needed to be focused for the next seventeen weeks. She did not want him to worry about her mental state. She couldn't be a distraction to him while he was undercover in the lion's den.

*

During a night-time walk through their neighbourhood, they had come across a community centre. By the looks of it, the centre had a brand new notice board with information about classes and activities that took place there. One in particular had caught Cassandra's eye: an art class for beginners. Art was something she had enjoyed when she was younger, much younger. Being the next Picasso had been her dream when all her classmates wanted to become rock stars or princesses. In fact, she was sure she could have been the next Picasso if it wasn't for her maths teacher. She had advised against pursuing the artist's dream and convinced her of the little use a qualification in art had. Cassandra had listened. It was probably the only academic decision she regretted.

She took the email address from the poster and messaged the group to sign up as soon as they were home. For a moment, she relived the daydreams she had fifteen years ago when she was sure becoming an artist was what she was born to do. Since leaving school, she hadn't been particularly interested in art but it was something to do and a way to meet people in town. Her first class would be in two days and all she had to bring was a sketchbook and a blank canvas. The centre provided everything else. A single class was nine dollars and a twelve-week pass was a hundred-and-fifty. She chose the latter. Even if it turned out to be awful, she figured it was something to get her out of the house.

*

The next morning they decided their day was not going to be about preparing for the training or the mission. Instead they would do something fun in the city. Neither of them had spoken about their feelings properly but it was clear that their cover relationship was more than just a cover. They had slept in the same bed since their trip to Glynco and had sex several times. Markus figured there was no need to talk about it if they were going to behave like a real couple anyway.

"What about the National Gallery of Art? It might give you some inspiration for your art class," Markus suggested when they were brainstorming ideas of things they could do on their last day together.

"Sounds like a good plan, but first I need a very big breakfast," she said, holding her stomach to emphasise her hunger.

"It's nearly half past twelve. We might as well call it lunch," he said while jumping out of bed and 'accidentally' taking the covers with him.

Initially she thought that it was merely him making a point to get going, but seeing the look on his face, she realised it was a cheeky attempt to get another glimpse of her body. It made her smile.

*

"Hi, how're you doing? I'm Marissa. Are you guys ready to order?" the young waitress with a genuine looking smile asked them.

Over the past two weeks they had eaten out several times, often feeling like the service was attentive, but so overly friendly that it felt fake. It was taking some adjustment to get used to.

"Good, thanks. I think we are. May I please have the

grilled cheese with sourdough, the Parma and Rocquefort salad and the soup of the day, please? Oh, and an orange juice to drink, please."

"And what would you like to drink, sir?" the waitress turned to Markus.

"That food was just for me," Cas cut in. "He still has to order his own."

The girl was shocked that Cas had ordered three meals for herself. "The portions are quite big here…"

"It's breakfast *and* lunch for me."

After both of them eating enough food for two days, it was a struggle to get into gear. Markus, especially, would have loved to just go home and spread out on the couch. But a plan had been made and he knew that once Cassandra had a plan, it was happening. Even his advanced negotiation skills wouldn't get him out of it. Unless a hurricane appeared out of this lovely, calm day, they were going to the gallery. What he did not know was the reason Cassandra was so intent on keeping them busy all day. It was the technique she had decided on to forget that he was leaving her so soon.

The only thing he was able to change about their day out was their mode of transport. He convinced Cas to get a taxi instead of the overcrowded and slow public transport. It wasn't particularly crowded on a Sunday afternoon but the excuse worked in his favour. All Markus wanted to do was to get comfy, relax a little and give the food a chance to settle before he was dragged around the gallery all afternoon.

Once they were in the cab, Markus started to feel like the universe was not on his side today. The taxi driver was a talker. He fired one question after another at them. Cas was too involved with her phone to answer and he didn't want to be rude, so he entertained the cabbie's questions for a good ten minutes. Then the driver asked him where he had bought his coat.

That was it. He had to get this man to stop talking. He pretended he was getting a call on his phone – even talking to himself for the next ten blocks was better than answering another useless question.

Suddenly Cassandra burst out laughing, so loudly Markus forgot what he was telling himself. She had just realised what he was doing and obviously found the lengths he would go to avoid the driver very funny. Markus rounded up his fake phone call and shoved the phone back into his pocket, sinking down in his seat and giving Cas a black look that she was laughing at him.

*

It was Monday 5 AM. Cassandra was wide awake even though they hadn't gone to bed until after midnight. Once they got back from their day out in the city, they quickly made the decision to just grab a bottle of wine and takeaway pizzas rather than to cook.

Cassandra was ordinarily a morning person and woke easily and full of energy. It was unusual for her to wake after less than five hours sleep though. She was nervous

– they were going to start their undercover life properly today. No more Cassandra and Markus. They were Natasha Connelly and Jonathan Black, a couple who had recently moved to Washington, DC for Jonathan's career. From now on, she was essentially a housewife who attended an art class a few times a week. The thought of her new life bored her already. Until the training programme was over, she had nothing to do except exist as a woman with a rubbish name.

She had been awake now for nearly half an hour, going through all the different scenarios of the future in her head. The thought of them finding out Markus's real identity kept on blaring in her mind. What would she do if they found out he was a spy? Would she be able to save him? She was worried. The first day was definitely going to be the riskiest. According to the paperwork, he was all clear. None of the people he trained with in Glynco should be at this training facility, but she knew that the personnel could change without them knowing. Every time she thought about Markus in the White House alone, she felt queasy. It was not a feeling she was used to. She had never worried about Markus in dangerous situations before. Not like this. She would feel better if her role could allow her to be in there with him.

Normally she would have woken Markus up by now but she figured he would need all the sleep he could get on his first day. By now it was 5:45 AM, only fifteen more minutes until the alarms would go off.

Fifteen minutes on paper might seem like nothing,

but when lying in the same position rethinking the same thoughts over and over again, each minute can feel like an hour. She looked at the clock again, and it had barely moved even though she had been trying to wait as long as possible before checking. She laughed to herself. She knew how impatient she was being. On any other day she would have quietly got up to make some tea or watch some television but this was the last morning they would wake up together. At least for the next seventeen weeks.

She was sick of waiting. She began to toss and turn, exaggerating her movements to make sure he wouldn't be able to sleep through it. She had woken him ten minutes before his alarm was meant to sound. He looked at her groggily in accusation.

"I know you said not to wake you, but I thought we could both use the extra ten minutes before the next seventeen weeks," she said while firmly pressing herself to the side of his chest for some morning cuddles.

As soon as he felt her warmth against his body, any irritation he might have been feeling vanished. He couldn't be mad at her for this.

The morning went by too quickly and too soon she was waving goodbye to him, emotional like any real girlfriend would be.

10

Even though Cas was alone now the day seemed to pass by just as fast as the last few days together had. All she had managed to do today was buy a canvas for her class and it was already time to make her way to the community centre. It was a quarter past seven and it was starting to get dark outside. Cas loved spring but she couldn't wait for her first American summer. She was already dreaming about the late nights she and Markus would spend in their garden in a couple of months, stargazing, drinking wine and enjoying each other's company.

She decided to walk to her class. Even though it was already getting dark, it was still relatively mild out for this time of the year. She was a little bit nervous, but in a good way. Cas had not painted in years, so the idea of meeting a group of new people and doing something she was probably no good at made her feel jittery.

Walking to the community centre was the right decision as all the parking spaces in front of the building were taken. Cas smiled when she saw that two of the spaces could have been free if the people owning those massive SUV's learned to park properly. She knew that this would have irritated her endlessly if she had driven tonight.

Two women were standing in front of the building and chatting. Seeing that they were too busy laughing and talking to notice her at first, Cassandra jumped in with a nervous, "Hi." She said it so ridiculously quietly that she must have sounded like a small shy child.

"Oh, hi! Sorry. Can I help you?" one of the ladies said.

"I'm looking for Leanne. We've been in touch over email about the art class here."

"You must be Natasha. Hi, I'm Leanne and this is Carrie Williams. It's nice to meet you," she said while shaking Natasha's hand.

"Nice to meet you too," Cas said, giving the ladies a warm smile. She could have guessed that the hippie lady was the teacher. She definitely looked like an artist with her rainbow hair-bands and flared jeans. Carrie looked like a housewife that only came to these classes to socialise. *She must own one of those terribly parked cars*, Cas thought to herself. She seemed almost too polished and put-together. Usually she would have stayed away from someone like Carrie, she was getting vibes she did not necessarily like.

"I need to get a couple of things out of my car. Carrie, could you show Natasha around and get her settled in?"

Carrie gave her a nod and took Cas inside the cosy

community centre. Cas decided to give Carrie a chance – not that she had much of a choice now that she was her personal guide.

The building was old and could definitely have used some TLC but there was a nice feeling about it. The room they were using had tables set up in a big U-shape and had a little kitchen in the corner with a kettle and coffee machine. The walls were decorated with paintings and other artwork. The building reminded Cas of the Girl Scouts Club she was once a part of, both had the same rustic cosy look to them.

"Where are you from?" the curly blonde-haired woman asked her.

"I'm part Spanish, part British, but I've spent most of my life in Amsterdam. We only moved here a couple of weeks ago," Cas said. As soon as the last word was out of her mouth she realised what she was saying. It was her first day alone and she had already messed up her cover story. She inwardly cursed herself before quickly adding, "My boyfriend and I were staying in San Francisco before we moved here. We moved for his work. How about you?"

"Born and raised in DC and I don't think I will ever leave," Carrie said smiling proudly.

In the end, Cassandra was actually glad she had met Carrie first. She was different to what she had expected and even made an effort to introduce her to everyone in the class. Including Cassandra, four women and two men were taking part tonight. They all seemed nice but Carrie was definitely her favourite by the end of the class. It surprised her how fast she had warmed to the woman in just an hour and a half. Carrie turned out to be the opposite of the obnoxious housewife she expected her to be. Apparently she just liked to dress like one. Cas thought that it was Carrie's down-to-earth persona, when she appeared at first to be anything but, that made her like her.

"Thanks for coming tonight and remember, Thursday's class will be at ten in the morning this week. I hope you enjoyed tonight, Tash, and well done. You've got some great ideas."

Cas was unsure if Leanne just said this to make her come back or if it was actually true. Either way, she didn't really care, she had decided to keep coming back the moment she realised she and Carrie really clicked. They talked about travelling, holidays and their adventures. Carrie talked a lot, but in a good way. She was one of those people who were able to fill any silence.

Carrie suggested they go to a bar which was equal distance from their houses. Cas was over the moon to have met a potential friend during her first class. It was even better she only lived a couple of streets away. She just needed to keep reminding herself to stick to her cover story, especially now that alcohol was about to be involved.

*

The bar was not like anything Cas was expecting. She had expected the stylish blonde to take her somewhere modern and cool. Instead, the bar was old and dark and reminded her a lot of the neighbourhood pub she went to as an exchange student in London. The average age of the customers of that London bar was sixty-plus but they did cocktails, and the prices were an amazing bargain.

There was only a handful of people in the bar when they entered: an elderly couple, two middle-aged men and the young female bartender. The men looked over when they walked in but went back to their conversation. The couple were clearly practically part of the bar's furnishings, they looked like they were best friends with the bartender.

Cas struggled with lying to her new friend because of the great connection between them. It felt like she was lying to someone she had known for years. After a while, she realised she was falling into a routine of changing the subject whenever a question didn't suit her. It almost seemed like Carrie was on to her porky pies when she kept asking questions about San Francisco and their move here.

"Do you live with someone or is it just you?" Cas asked as she grabbed her dirty martini off the table to take a sip before it was her turn to talk again.

"Me and my daughter. My husband, Michael, passed away nearly four years ago. My mom comes and stays with us a few days a week to watch Jordan whenever I've got stuff to do. I don't know what I would do without her support. I never thought I'd be raising a child by myself. Michael was the one that really wanted children. He would have been better at this."

Cas could see that her friend's eyes were starting to water. "I'm sure you're doing great," she said as she put her hand over Carrie's. She wasn't sure what else to say and hoped the comforting gesture was enough.

"What about you? Is it just the boyfriend or do you have kids?" Carrie said, forcing herself to move past the teary moment.

"No, we don't. It's just the two of us. Or just me, actually, since he's away right now. Neither of us wants kids, at least not yet. He wants to focus on his career for now and I have to figure out what to focus on. Maybe Leanne is right and art is my calling," she joked.

After finishing another two rounds of drinks, it was time for Carrie to get home to relieve her mom. The timing was perfect as Markus had just texted Cas to see if she was ready for a quick debrief. She replied and told him to call in fifteen minutes. That would give her just enough time to get home and make a cup of tea.

*

Exactly fifteen minutes later, the phone rang.

"Tash? Oh hey sweetie, how are you?" They had agreed to let the other know they could not talk freely by using their cover names.

"I'm good, very good actually. Slightly tipsy maybe. How was your day?"

"It was good, interesting. Everyone seems friendly. All going smoothly so far. I don't have much to report yet but by the sounds of it, you do? You're tipsy? I thought you were going to an art class," he laughed.

81

"Well, I was. I did. I made a friend. Carrie. She's great. We're going for breakfast before our class on Thursday morning. She…ugh I forget. I think I need to keep this short. The bathroom is calling my name…"

"Okay. Sweet dreams for later."

"Uh huh. Yeah. Oh God…okay, bye."

As soon as she hung up, she knew that Markus was laughing at her at the other end of the line. He knew that she was a lightweight and that it wasn't just that she needed the toilet. Her stomach was calling for the bathroom, a sink, bucket, anything.

After the unpleasant visit to the bathroom, Cas crawled to her bed not understanding how she could suddenly feel this drunk. She only felt tipsy when she had left the bar. She felt too ill to even care about taking off her clothes or finding her pyjamas. As soon as she was horizontal, the room started spinning so much she had to use the old foot on the floor trick.

"Drunk enough to feel dreadful but not drunk enough to pass out. Fucking great," she mumbled when she turned over for the tenth time in five minutes. She had rarely been this drunk before. It almost felt like the moment she had woken up feeling nauseous after the surgery on her leg. Suddenly, she felt sick again.

She got up as fast as she could to go back to the bathroom but as soon as she stood up, she felt dizzy. She was so dizzy she could barely walk straight. Her sight was getting blurry. She lost her balance just as she reached the bathroom door and she fell.

Everything went black.

An odd sensation was going through her body. The nauseous feeling was gone but she couldn't see or move, it felt like someone had hit her on the back of the head with force. She couldn't move.

She lay there for what felt like hours. Then she heard a noise: the sound of glass breaking or a window being smashed. She could hear footsteps downstairs. She tried to scream but her lips wouldn't move when she tried to make a sound. She was terrified.

The sound of the footsteps gradually disappeared. All she could hear was the sound of her own breath panting through the lips she had no control over. Had someone poisoned her? Was she dying? Once more, she tried to scream or move. Nothing happened. She was helpless. The panic she was feeling was overwhelming. She fainted.

11

Markus had messaged Cassandra several times throughout the day but had not received anything back. He was starting to get worried. This was unlike her. She usually replied to messages very promptly. At first he assumed that she was having a lie-in because of the hangover she must have but when he still couldn't get through to her by noon, he knew that something was not right. He felt trapped and helpless, not being able to go and make sure she was okay. They would definitely not let him go unless he had a better reason than just a hunch, and sneaking out unnoticed was also impossible. The training centre was like Fort Knox.

His day had gone well apart from not hearing back from his partner. The guys that were training with him were nice, the food was all right and the first two days of training so far had been a piece of cake. Once they finished

their day's training, Markus sprinted back to his ro
check his phone. Still nothing. He tried to call – the pl
was ringing but she still wasn't picking up. He contacted
AJ to see if he had heard from her. Nothing. Something
was definitely wrong.

He started to go through all the possible scenarios in
his head. Maybe she was somewhere with no reception.
Maybe she dropped and broke her phone. Maybe she'd
lost it somewhere. Maybe she'd been mugged and they'd
taken her phone. Maybe there was a fire. Then he suddenly
had the horrible image of the house being on fire with a
drunk and disoriented Cas inside. He cursed himself for
having such horrible thoughts and the way he'd let his
imaginings escalate.

Just then his training mate, Carl, walked in. "Jonathan,
dinner's ready. We're all waiting for you."

His reply to Carl came out rather short and coupled with
a grunt. It probably sounded rude even though he had no
intention to be. His worries about Cassandra made it hard
to concentrate or think properly. He made it a point to try
to socialise with the guys during dinner, especially Carl.
He didn't want him to think that he was a rude, antisocial
dickhead.

Apart from all the training you would expect, a
large part of the programme made him feel like he was
attending etiquette school. It was a lot of rules and
traditions, only for grown adults. Markus would normally
be all right with rules and authority, but he was currently
preoccupied.

As soon as dinner was done, he rushed back to his phone. To his relief there was a message in his inbox. It was from Cas.

I'm ok. Speak tomorrow.

Markus was confused. Cas had never done this before. He tried to call her immediately but she did not pick up. This was getting stranger and stranger. Cas never took so long to reply and when she did it was never so short, even if it was just a text. The tone was all wrong as well – she always started with a 'hey, hola,' or something and she always signed off with an 'x'.

Markus didn't sleep much that night. He could not help thinking about all the reasons she could have for not speaking to him. Was it something he had done or said? At some point at two in the morning his thoughts wandered off so far that he even started to rethink their last phone call and their last day together, wracking his brain to see if he had done something to upset her. He could not think of anything.

It was four before he finally fell asleep, his brain exhausted from thinking the same things over and over again. The negative thoughts crossing his mind gave him dreams of the worst possible scenarios.

12

Cas woke up still lying on the hallway floor. It was now the afternoon. She was sure that she had been drugged the night before. At least she was able to move again, though all her limbs hurt and her head was pounding. She made to go downstairs to check what had happened but as soon as she got up to head towards the stairs, she knew she would not be able to make it all the way. Moving any part of her body still hurt too much. She just about managed to slowly hobble to her room. She needed to rest.

Once she got into her bed she picked up her phone and saw Markus's missed calls and messages. When she noticed what time it was she realised she had been on the floor for more than seventeen hours. She wanted to call Markus but she felt too weak even for that. A quick text saying she was all right would have to do for now. What the hell had she been poisoned with? All she knew was that she felt knackered even though she had just slept for seventeen hours. There was not much she could do except sleep some more and hope she would wake up feeling better.

*

She was relieved when she woke up to her alarm the next day at eight in the morning. She had slept for another full twelve hours but at least she was able to turn over and switch off her alarm. Once she got up it was clear that the pain was not fully gone but it was certainly a lot better. She was able to stand up, walk around and talk. The unbearable paralyzing pain had been replaced with a dull ache in her muscles that only hurt when she moved. It reminded her of the sort of muscle pain she would get after going clubbing, dancing and hanging upside down on a pole when she was nineteen. There was a club in Soho she used to go to with her friends when she lived in London. Every time they went there she would be sore all over for at least two days. Hopefully this pain would be gone in two days as well.

When she checked her phone again, she realised how worried Markus had been. He had sent several texts, left voicemails and there were a dozen missed calls. She felt horrible about not giving some more information last night but she had not felt capable of it. She tried to call him back but it was after eight and his training had already started. She left him a voice message instead telling him what had happened. At least what she remembered of it.

She was almost finished explaining when she looked out the window she had made her way towards while she'd been talking. "FUCK! The car. The car's gone!" That was the last thing Markus would hear of her message.

She thought back to the night before and remembered the sound of glass breaking. It was time to go downstairs and check what was left of their home.

*

Walking down the stairs was nerve-wracking. Cassandra did not understand how this could have happened on her first night alone. She tried to remember everything that people had said or done that night but nothing felt bizarre or suspicious. Everyone at the art class seemed all right, she had not noticed anyone acting strange in the bar and she never felt like anyone was following her. Noticing suspicious behaviour or someone watching you is something you get trained to do with ICU. It gets to be an instinctive habit that you do no matter where you are, like scanning the room when you first enter. No one had stood out in the bar. The only people she had noted were the two middle-aged men who she'd initially thought had been eyeing her and Carrie up. It was possible they had been looking her up and down for a different reason. Maybe they had sized her up to see if she would make a good target to rob.

Luckily the damage was not as bad as she feared. One of the panes of glass on the back door was smashed. The car was gone, the massive flat-screen, her Nutri-bullet and a couple of other smaller items. They had obviously targeted her for her brand new Jeep Cherokee and just taken the opportunity with the other items while they were there. Was this a coincidence? Or had someone chosen her for a reason? How had they drugged her? And with what? Cassandra had so many questions but no answers.

She knew she had to do some investigating to find out the truth but she also knew that protocol would not allow her to. ICU would just get her a new car and make her carry on like nothing had happened. The mission came before anything. Hell, they would have probably just replaced her if she had died last night. She was going to tell them about the break-in and the stolen car but she decided to leave out the part about her being drugged. She would be free to investigate on her own this way and find the bastards that had done this to her.

Her plan was to speak to Carrie and then go back to the bar to check out their CCTV footage but Carrie's phone went straight to voicemail. She wanted to go to the bar but as soon as she started walking down the road she started to feel rubbish again. She decided against it and turned around. Her own reflection gave her a fright when she saw herself in a shiny sports car parked on the street. She couldn't remember looking this pale since the time she had food poisoning. She had been the one to poison herself and Markus – it wasn't on purpose, obviously, but they both were horribly sick for days. The only time she might have looked worse was after her accident in Russia but her recovery time there was spent mostly unconscious. It almost didn't count because it didn't feel real. She had been out for weeks and by the time she was conscious enough to care what she looked like, she had already been on the mend.

After arranging to get the back door fixed, she was tired again. Luckily the joiner was not available until the next day because she did not think she could handle that today. She decided that the best remedy to get better was more sleep, so she switched the television in her room to a random program and lightly dozed off for a few hours.

*

The sound of her phone ringing gave her a fright. When she turned over and picked up her phone, she realised that it was late. She must have properly fallen into a deep sleep again. Sleeping this much was unlike her – she usually didn't need more than five or six hours a night. What the hell did they drug her with? Cas had tried drugs before but nothing she had ever tried had made her feel like this.

It was Markus calling. Apparently whatever they had done to her affected her concentration as much as her sleeping habits. Her mind was so preoccupied with her own thoughts that she had let the phone go to voicemail again. Instead of listening to the message she called him straight back. After all, she knew exactly what his voicemail would say and it was understandable. She had told him what had happened briefly – she hadn't told him everything – but it was enough to worry him.

"Markus, I'm so sorry," she said immediately once he picked up. She should have waited to see if he addressed her by Cas or Tash but she didn't give him a chance. Instead she spent the next twenty minutes explaining everything that had happened since he had left Monday morning.

She told him about her art class, her new friend, the pub they went to, her walk home and everything that had happened since the moment she had head-butted the floor. She was relieved when Markus agreed with her plan of speaking to Carrie and checking the CCTV. For a moment, she was worried his concern would make him demand she stick to protocol.

"Good night, Cas. I miss you. Be safe."

13

It was six AM, Thursday, and the sun was shining. Cas was wide awake and feeling like herself again. It was the first time she woke up before her alarm since the events of Monday night. It took her two whole days to recover from whatever she had been drugged with. Her initial guess was horse tranquilizer given how she had hit the floor on Monday but the intense pain she had been in after waking was unusual. She had never heard of anyone showing the same symptoms she had exhibited. It must either be some horrible new drug or a nasty cocktail of several to have incapacitated her for so many days.

Cas knew that the only way of finding out what rubbish the culprits had put into her body was by finding out who did this to her. She was determined to find the motherfuckers. Her protocol told her not to but ICU did not have to find out if she did things properly without leaving a trail.

She decided that it was the universe's way of giving her something to do other than being stuck here as a suburban housewife. Being Markus's handler and doing this little investigation were two things she could easily combine. Cas had always been a star at multitasking.

After tossing and turning for half an hour she had made a plan. It was time to get up and start her investigation. Cas grabbed her phone from the nightstand and realised that Carrie had finally got back to her. The text was short:

> Sorry was out all day without my phone!
> You coming to class tomorrow? Give me
> a call before if not. xo C

Besides sending Carrie a text she had also left a voicemail just before going to bed. She had explained what had happened to her on Monday night...or had she? Carrie was making no mention of it. Cas was getting confused – was her memory playing tricks on her? Had she left that voicemail as she thought she did? She impulsively tried to call Carrie to get this sorted out. Only once the phone connected and started to ring did her eye glance at the clock. *Shit!* She quickly hung up and wrote a text apologising for not realising how early it was when she tried to call. She asked if they were still on for breakfast before their class and left it at that until she could speak to her in person. She hoped Carrie still wanted to do breakfast – she needed to get to the bottom of this.

Cas was sick of waiting around. She should probably wait until the bar opened and explain her situation but she could not stand sitting around thinking any longer. She had done that for days while her body was too weak. Now that she was stronger, she needed to do something. She was going down to that bar and have a nose around. She was already disobeying ICU protocol, a little break-in was no big deal. No one was ever going to find out. Not even ICU. Her training had taught her how to blend in, be somewhere unseen and not leave any evidence behind.

For a second she thought about messaging Markus to update him on her plan but she thought better of it. He would not be able to help her anyway, not until he was done with his training.

Black joggers, a dark jumper and trainers would do. At least if she ran into anyone they would just think that she was a fitness freak going for a 6 AM run before work.

She felt confident that the footage she would find in the bar would give her answers, or at least some leads. She started jogging any time she saw someone approaching, just to make her fitness nut cover believable. She jogged the route through the streets to the bar, or what she thought was the route. Once again her mind was playing tricks on her. She was so certain that she knew the way, she had not checked the maps on her phone – after all, the bar had not been far. After fifteen minutes of running through the neighbourhood, lost, Cas headed for the community centre to see if she could retrace the exact steps she and Carrie had taken.

Finally. It worked. She could see the little bar at the end of the street.

Luckily the entrance to the bar was on a long and quiet street and it was early enough that no one was around. It only took her a few seconds to jimmy the lock and leave it in such a way that no one would notice it had been touched. It made her appreciate all the useful things she had learned with ICU. If they sacked her for this, she could always become a locksmith...or a thief. The training to become an ICU agent was so long and extensive that it almost felt like you had learned a dozen professions while doing it.

As soon as Cas pushed open the heavy door the alarm started beeping. Without batting an eye, she held up the gadget she had tucked into her sleeve up to the alarm panel. After two more beeps, the alarm was silenced. On top of gaining her entry, all record of her disabling the alarm was wiped. As far as the system was concerned, nothing had happened and the alarm was still in place. All courtesy of ICU.

Monday night's CCTV footage proved to be nothing but frustrating. The cameras were pointed on the entrance, the bar area and the hallway leading to the smoking area. The footage was pretty much useless. The table she and Carrie were at was in a blind spot of all the cameras. She had hoped to see someone put something in her drink or someone who might have seen something suspicious. If only they had sat in the booth she suggested when they first entered the bar, they would have been in plain sight of the cameras there. According to the footage, only two people could have been near enough to spike her: one was the young bartender, the other was Carrie. Cas was confused. She could not remember being near anyone for any length of time that night except for Carrie. She decided to take the footage with her anyway. Maybe a background check on all the punters would help her uncover the truth.

Her heart stopped after hearing a noise coming from upstairs. Someone was in the building. It was the sound of someone knocking over an empty glass. Maybe the cleaner? She hadn't noticed anyone coming in because the monitors had been displaying Monday's footage. When she quickly switched them back, everything looked the same as before. She quickly finished copying the footage and got out the knife she had taken with her. Just in case. She was not planning on using it…as long as everything went to plan.

With the knife in one hand and a torch in the other, she quietly left the basement office. The old wooden stairs were a nightmare – no matter how hard Cas tried to make little to no noise, they squeaked and creaked with every step she made. She stopped at the top of the stairs and had a good look in every corner of the bar. Nothing. Her heartbeat was starting to slow when suddenly something came flying at her from one of the booths. Cas couldn't help letting out a short scream even as she nimbly turned towards her attacker, ready to face them head on.

It was a cat.

A bloody cat. She let the intruder and herself out whilst shaking her head. In the past, even when a gunman was coming right at her she had never let out a scream like she just did. The lack of back-up definitely made Cas more nervous. Normally she had Markus there to have her back whether it was a gunman or a cat flying at her. She would have never screamed with him around. He never would have stopped going on about it. Markus would have taken the piss out of her for days, at least.

The adrenaline was still racing through her body while she walked home. She had missed this – the excitement of being on a mission. It's a specific rush you got from doing things you weren't technically supposed to be doing but you still knew you were on the side of the right. It was good she had not left any later. The streets were starting to fill up with people walking their dogs, going to work or taking their kids to school. Cassandra was secretly pleased. The footage did not give her the answers she was hoping for, and she may have been terrified by a stray cat, but she had just completed her first solo mission in the United States of America successfully.

By the time she got back to the house, Carrie had messaged her. She could meet but only for a quick coffee before class. That would have to do. A half-hour coffee date was all she would need to interrogate her new friend. Now all she could do was hope that Carrie knew something useful.

*

They agreed to meet in a café straight across from the

community centre as they would not have much time before the start of the class. Almost every table in the café was taken. It surprised Cas that it was so busy on a Thursday morning. This must be the place to be for all the housewives that don't have anything better to do during the week when the kids are at school, Cas thought to herself. Her thoughts made her laugh a little when she realised she was one of those women now. Well, minus the kids.

As a teenager, she had always imagined that she would have children round about the age she was now. Since starting at ICU, that thought had been pushed to the back of her mind more and more over the years. The thought of having kids seemed unrealistic now. Working for the agency had made her image of her future change massively. Since working for ICU, she now assumed she would be an active agent until she was forty or fifty. After that, she would retire on a sunny beach in some remote corner of the world.

"Tash, over here."

It took her a few seconds to spot Carrie, the table she was sitting at was hidden by a double trouble buggy. Plus her hair was darker and had been straightened – at least if the memory she had of Carrie being a curly-haired blonde was correct. So many thoughts and memories were blurry since Monday night that she was doubting herself.

"Carrie. Hi, how are you? You look great," she said, making a gesture towards Carrie's head.

"Thank you. I just got it done yesterday…Just felt like a change, I guess. How have you been?"

Relieved by the fact that she was not going entirely crazy, it was time to get down to business. "I've been awful, to be completely honest with you. That's why I needed to talk to you. This is going to sound crazy…but I think I was drugged and robbed after we had drinks on Monday night. I have no idea what I was drugged with but I passed out on my hallway floor and was incapable of doing anything for about two days. They smashed my back door window and stole my car. A few other things are missing as well." Cas took a deep breath in the silence that sat between them. The look on Carrie's face was full of disbelief and concern.

"Oh my God! Are you okay now? Have you been to the police?"

Cas sighed. She had planned to ask questions, not have to answer them. "I'm okay, just a little shaken I guess. Can you remember anything odd happening Monday night? Was there anyone in the bar acting strange? Was my drink unattended at all when I went to the bathroom? I need to figure out what happened. Please, dig as deep as you can. Any little detail could help."

14

Markus's first week of training was over and everything had gone smoothly, especially compared to Cassandra's first week alone. As far as everyone in the training facility was concerned, he was Jonathan Black. The stress of being found out was slowly starting to fade. For once it seemed like fortune was on his side. No one had recognised him or seemed to suspect anything at all. Markus felt like he was becoming more like the real Jonathan every day.

The training itself was a piece of cake. The hardest part for Markus was being away from Cassandra. Before this American adventure started they had been separated for months while she was recovering. He had missed her during that time, of course, but nothing like what he was experiencing now. He wasn't sure he had missed anyone as much. It made him wonder what their relationship would be like once this mission was over. They would be sent home and no longer required to pretend to be a couple – though Markus was relatively sure neither of them were pretending anymore, at least not since the trip to Glynco.

Today the training would take them off-site. All they had been told was that the bus would depart in one hour. No one knew where they were going or what they were going to do. That was the way the service worked. The higher-ups thought it was crucial for potential secret service officers to be flexible and adaptable. It was all part of the training regimen, one that Markus did not necessarily agree with. He liked having a schedule. For now all he could do was suck it up though. He had started the countdown of the seventeen weeks like a prisoner, making little scores on the side of his bed. Each mark meant he was one day closer to seeing Cas.

As soon as he got back to his room after the morning's briefing, he tried to call Cas. They had told him that this off-site exercise could last anywhere from three hours to three days. Phones were obviously not allowed, so he did not know when he would be able to contact her again.

"Hey, I was just on the phone arranging to pick up the new car in a few days. How are you?" she sounded out of breath.

"I'm good but I don't have much time. We're doing some off-site training, which could take up to three days. There's no way of knowing. They love keeping us in the dark here. Hold on, I'll just put you on speaker while I'm getting ready. We're leaving in five.

102

How're you getting on? Any news?" he questioned, as he put his phone down to start packing.

"All fine, no news really. The new car is going to be a replica of the last, so you won't even notice it was ever gone. My background search on all the people in the bar was useless. They're all completely ordinary law-abiding people as far as I can tell. I'll have to put my investigation on hold and go back to becoming the next Picasso, I guess," she said smiling, knowing that he would be able to pick up on her rueful smile over the phone.

"I've got to go, Cas. I'm not sure when I'll get the chance to contact you next. Have a good week."

"Good luck."

"Bye."

"I miss you, Markus."

"Jonathan, hurry up. We're leaving," a voice cut in. Carl had come to hurry him up and was standing outside the door. Markus quickly grabbed the phone, switched it off and chucked it in the bag he was leaving behind. With his rucksack strapped on his back, he and Carl made their way towards the car park. After walking in silence for most of the way, Carl suddenly stopped, "Who was that you were talking to? I could swear I heard her call you Markus…"

Carl had obviously spent the walk contemplating whether he should say something or not. Markus told him it was his girlfriend Natasha but the look on his face remained sceptical.

"It's just a nickname she has for me," Markus tried to explain. Carl did not look any more convinced.

Markus had mostly kept to himself over the last week, which in hindsight might have caused suspicion among the other trainees. He had barely told them anything about himself – or Jonathan, rather. "It's a silly thing. We were both in this play in high school and we started calling each other by the characters' names even outside of practice. It was a silly inside joke. Now it's just habit," he quickly improvised.

"Fair enough." Carl seemed less intent now, which comforted Markus that he believed him. "I was in a play in high school too. Lion King. Rafiki. Lots of singing and dancing up a tree." At this, Markus allowed himself to laugh – partly at the image of Carl acting like a monkey, but mostly out of relief he was still in the clear.

15

"**M**orning, Leanne. How are you this wonderful morning?" Cas said with a big smile on her face.

"Good morning dear. I'm good, thanks. You're in a very chipper mood today…and very early too," she said whilst checking the time on her watch.

"Just picked up my new car this morning, that's why. I never thought I would miss having a car in just a couple of days. Apparently I'm more dependent on it than I thought. Instead of going home for breakfast, I ended up cruising around the neighbourhood for the past half hour," she said sheepishly.

Picking up the new car was not the only reason for Cas being early. This class was pretty much the only social interaction she had apart from catching up with Markus over the phone. Even though it was only her fourth class today, she had grown very fond of everyone who attended, especially Carrie – they had become so close so quickly. Carrie and her daughter, Jordan, had even been over for brunch on Saturday. Cas was impressed when she first met her – a well-mannered child is hard to come across these days. Carrie seems to have taught her well, but maybe too well, since Jordan seemed almost nervous at brunch and very careful about her behaviour. Cas didn't blame her for it though– she remembered how much she hated going to lunch with her mother's friends. Carrie, for her part, didn't seem to pay much attention to Jordan.

When Cassandra first started going to these classes it was purely for the social aspect but now that she knew what she was going to paint, she was focused on doing it as professionally as possible. She always did everything to the best of her abilities even if she did not particularly enjoy what she was doing. It was part of her personality and always had been. 'Being good enough is not good enough when you can be great,' had been her motto during high school. Even though she had been pretty even in high school, she had not always been well-liked or very popular. Cassandra thought a large part of that was because she was too driven and ambitious.

Painting itself was starting to become enjoyable now that her work was beginning to look half decent. Her first masterpiece was going to be a scene straight out of an African safari, starring a big elephant as the focus. Cas had a thing for elephants, she used to draw lots of them as a child and all that elephant drawing practice she had done years ago made her look like a natural talent now.

Of course, she did not let on this wasn't her first attempt – she quite liked getting praised for her seemingly natural talent.

Carrie came rushing in, out of breath, just after the class had started. There was only a couple of people there this Monday morning but Cas had kept the seat next to her occupied with one of her bags. The two had gotten so close over the last week and a half that Carrie automatically chucked her bag on the floor beside Cas because she knew that seat had her name on it. This friendship had started off so quickly but already felt so solid that it reminded Cas of the friendships she had when she was young. In school, especially primary school, people could become your best friend in a day. Admittedly those friendships often only lasted a day as well, but it would feel like it was for forever at the time. Cas had not made a new friend this easily since those days. She struggled with trusting people but she liked Carrie, a lot. She was probably the first person she was starting to trust since she had been teamed up with Markus. Even with him, it had taken her a while before she fully trusted him.

"This morning was such a struggle. Jordan was making a big fuss about everything. The moment she started crying because her breakfast wasn't on the right plate was the moment I was done with her BS. I told her that I was done with her moaning and went upstairs to get myself ready. And guess what? As I'm pulling my sweater over my head I hear this enormous crash! She tried to get the plate she wanted down but leaned on the shelf and the whole damn thing came down! I guess we'll be eating out of bowls until I have the time and money to get new ones," she sighed while burying her face in her hands.

"Oh no! Poor you. That sounds like a rubbish morning. I can lend some plates until you have time to replace them. I'm by myself for the foreseeable future anyway," Cas felt stupid but did not know what else to do but to make the offer. She knew it sounded silly but it was to stop herself from saying what was on her mind: *Note to self: just don't have children if you want your house to say clean and intact.* She kept her mouth shut and carried on painting the trunk of her elephant.

Attempting to cheer Carrie up, Cas began telling her about her own childhood and teenage years. Some of the stories were only half true or were slightly exaggerated but it put a smile on Carrie's face and made her think a little less about her own brat.

"My mum once got me this jumper which I thought was awful! Even worse, it was one of those horrible itchy ones. I remember one day when I was in Kindergarten, so maybe four or five years old, she made me wear it. We were doing crafts and I just decided to cut it, a giant hole so big it couldn't be fixed. Of course I pretended it was an accident. I think I even tried to blame her somehow. I was making something special for her, so it was kind of her fault I cut it…Believe me, your Jordan is a saint compared to some." That got Carrie laughing and she only stopped when her phone started ringing.

"Hold on. It's Jordan's school. I've got to take this,"

she said, getting up to leave the room. "Hello, yes, this is Carrie Williams speaking."

*

"She's not in class!" Carrie almost shouted when she came back in. "They called to ask if I forgot to let them know that she's ill. I dropped her off fifteen minutes before the start of class. I left her playing in the playground with her friends!"

Cas could see the panic in her friend's face as she grabbed her handbag and sprinted back out of the room, leaving the rest of her stuff behind.

"Carrie, wait! I'll drive you," Cas yelled whilst rushing out after her friend. "Where do you want to go first?" she said once they had both climbed into her brand new car.

"The teacher assured me that she's definitely not at school, so let's go to mine first."

Even keeping her eyes on the road, Cas could feel how nervous Carrie was. She could sense her racing heartbeat and see her sweating from the corner of her eye. *This must be a parent's worst nightmare*, she thought whilst trying to comfort her friend and assure her they would find her daughter.

Carrie swung the door open before the car had fully stopped and was already inside by the time Cas was done parking.

"She's not here!" she wailed with a teary voice. "We've got to go look at the school ourselves. Maybe she felt sick and is in one of the bathrooms. I'll call my mom right now in case she went there. I don't understand, she's usually such a good girl. She wouldn't just skip class."

After putting the school's address in the navigation system of Cas's car, Carrie called her mother. Cas could see her friend's eyes get watery again when she had to tell her that Jordan was missing. She wasn't at her grandmother's. Another dead end.

"Where could she be if she's not at school, home, or at my mother's?" Carrie was fully crying now and only managed to stop when they arrived at the school.

The principal was already waiting for them. Carrie had called to let them know that she was en route.

"Mr Duval, where is my daughter? I dropped her off right here, fifteen minutes before the start of class. She was playing with Amber and Claire when I left. Where is she?" Carrie yelled at the white-haired man.

"I'm sorry. She never made it to her class. We've searched the whole property and can't find her anywhere. Mrs Williams, I think it's time we call the police if you're certain she isn't at home."

Carrie suddenly did not have the energy to keep upright anymore. She sunk down and leant on one of the toy tractors in the playground, "Call the police? This can't be happening."

The principal offered to make the call and he walked off to his office to do so. Having a child go missing on his watch must be a low point of his career, Cas thought, as she watched the elderly man walk away.

He had even started tearing up as well when speaking to Carrie. To Cas, that was a sign he cared for Jordan, a sign that she could exclude him from a suspect list – for now. Cassandra had jumped from friend mode back into agent mode as soon as they were sure Jordan was missing. Jordan was not the type of child that would go off on her own – something bad must have happened.

Cas and Carrie searched the whole school again after Carrie managed to collect herself a little. Nothing. However, when walking around the grounds, Cas realised that the school had CCTV cameras inside and outside the building.

"The police will be here soon. Can I get you anything?" Mr Duval asked. He likely meant he could get them a tea or coffee, but Cas was not going to pass on the offer.

"You could get us to your CCTV room. We could check if there's any useful info on the tapes," she asked, giving the man a gentle, comforting smile.

"I did think to try but I can't manage to work the system. Maintenance is usually in charge of it but Pete is off today. The police will be here soon."

It did not take Cas long to convince the principal that she knew CCTV systems well enough to work even a complicated one. He was keen to wait on the police in case they accidently deleted footage that might be crucial as evidence. Cassandra persisted. Once Cassandra put her mind to something, she usually got what she wanted.

The quality of the images was poor but you could clearly see Carrie drop Jordan off at the entrance of the playground. They could see Jordan run off to her friends and after a moment, Carrie waves goodbye and drives away.

The tension in the room was palpable. All three of them crammed in the tiny dark room were silent, three hearts beating faster than any of them had in a long time. They surely were about to see something that would explain where Jordan was, but what? All three sets of eyes were focused entirely on the screens.

"Who is that woman?" Cas abruptly broke the silence, pointing to a lone person walking towards Carrie's daughter. Jordan's friends had already gone inside. The woman was wearing a baseball cap and shades. Unfortunately, the image quality was not good enough for much more than that. The footage showed Jordan talking to the woman for a few minutes. It then showed Jordan walking away from the playground with the strange woman. Out of sight.

Carrie started crying but Cas was too busy to comfort her friend this time. Her priority was to find Jordan, so she did what she would normally do when investigating a case. She rewound the footage in case they had missed something important. She rewatched it again. And again.

"The police are here," the receptionist interrupted the trio with a knock on the door.

Carrie immediately got up to go speak to the police and was surprised that Cas made no move.

"I'm going over the footage again. I'll catch up with you in a minute," Cas reassured her. She did not need to watch it again just now but she wanted to make a copy of it before the police got there. She knew that the police would not allow it once they got their hands on the evidence. That was something she had gotten used to over the years. The police did not like civilians investigating or getting involved in their cases and, at least as far as they knew, Cas was a civilian. A lot of the time when ICU sent out a team on a mission, the police would be working on the same case without even knowing ICU agents were involved. There had been countless times that agents would feed the police a missing piece of evidence to solve a case, letting them think they had solved the mystery themselves. It was easier that ways because, of course, ICU did not officially exist.

Cas knew that she had to stay ahead of the police investigation if she wanted to be able to find Jordan quickly. After making a copy, she found Carrie speaking to the police officers. She introduced herself but then politely excused herself. Cas felt bad about being a rubbish friend, especially since the look on Carrie's face screamed for a shoulder to lean on. She made up some excuse about stomach cramps and needing the bathroom, but luckily no one questioned her sudden ailment, giving her time and space to work. While Carrie and the principal showed the officers the CCTV footage, Cas was already on the other side of the street checking if there could be any other cameras that may have caught Jordan and the woman as they walked away from the school.

The only shop with a camera pointing towards the street was a small tobacconist's. The camera looked ancient and

Cas had her doubts whether it was a working camera and not just there for show.

"Hi, how are you? What can I help you with today?" the short old man behind the counter said as she entered the shop. He looked like a cross between Santa Claus and a Hell's Angels biker.

"Sorry, I'm not actually here to buy anything but I wonder if you can help me…My car got broken into this morning and it looks like the camera outside your shop is pointing directly towards where it was parked." Before Cas even had a chance to ask, the old man offered to take her downstairs with a wave of his hand. *Obviously not much of a talker,* she thought to herself as she followed him down the narrow staircase.

"Do you know roughly what time?" he asked whilst logging into the CCTV system.

"Between eight and nine this morning, I think. Thank you."

Suddenly they heard the sound of the brass doorbell chime from upstairs.

"Excuse me, I'll be right back."

Inside, Cas was almost jumping with excitement. This could not have worked out any better. The old man had logged into the system and left her right in front of it. Alone.

*

Two more police cars were just arriving when Cas crossed

the street going back towards the school. She was planning on coming up with an excuse to get out of there as soon as possible. She would just lie about still having stomach issues since the night she had been drugged, even though it was nearly two weeks ago now. She found Carrie and offered to pick up her mother and bring her to her for the support but Carrie declined. She assured her that she was available over the phone if she needed her. As expected, she ended up sounding like a bit of an ass. Probably the last thing a parent needs when their child goes missing is a friend that thinks so much of the situation that they offer up only support over the phone.

As soon as Cas was through the door of her house, she sprinted up the stairs and got her laptop. She thought she had seen something when copying the tobacconist's CCTV footage to her thumb drive. Something small in the background but that could be a big help to finding Jordan and bringing her home. Even though she was not meant to get herself involved, Cassandra knew that this was the mission she had been waiting for. What agent could stand being a full-time housewife as a mission? Not Cassandra Young. She needed action and excitement. Otherwise, life just seemed a little dull.

The CCTV footage did not show as much as she hoped for, but it did confirm something strange was going on. The images showed Jordan and the woman walking down the street beside the school. Near the end of the street, it looked like another person joined them and at that point Jordan seemed to refuse to continue walking.

The woman grabbed her arm and they all got into a vehicle together. The part that bothered Cas the most was that Jordan had walked alongside this woman as if she had known her for years. What did this stranger say to her to gain her trust so easily at first? What if she wasn't a stranger? Cas suddenly had a strange feeling going through her body, one that she could not explain. She told herself that Carrie would have recognised the woman if it was someone they knew. She decided to make it a point to ask her anyway, though not just now.

She worried whether sending the CCTV footage to ICU's tech team would be a terrible idea. No, it was most definitely a terrible idea, but she could use the help of an expert to analyse the footage. It could help save Jordan. If certain people at work found out what she was doing, she would risk being pulled from her original mission. She would not be able to help find Jordan then, not to mention she would let Markus down. She imagined what Markus's reaction would be if he found out she had got herself effectively suspended. He would be devastated and she would not be allowed back in the field any time soon. It was too risky. She would have to find another way.

Cassandra remembered Markus working together closely with Interpol years ago when they first met. There was someone named Barry that he still spoke to over the phone now and again. She could always tell it was Barry he was speaking to because Markus always put on a French European accent when it was him. She assumed it had something to do with his cover story with Barry.

They had always sounded like they were close. Maybe he could help her now. The last she had heard, Barry was still working for Interpol as a technical analyst, but she would have to tell Markus what was going on. He would know what to do or who to call, whether it was Barry or one of the other contacts they had made over the years.

16

Jordan had been missing for a whole day now. Cassandra managed to get in touch with Markus late last night. At first he was not happy about what she was getting herself into but eventually understood after some persuading and sweet-talking. Markus sometimes was a stickler for rules but he also understood Cas and knew she needed to do this. He agreed to contact Barry after she told him her other option was asking ICU tech for help, which he knew was a horrible idea.

"I'll see what I can do. Just don't let anyone at ICU get wind of what you're doing. They'll put you on the first plane back if they find out," he had said in a strict parental tone.

Determined to do whatever it took, Cas was on her way to the school early in the morning. Her plan was to walk the same direction the vehicle had driven in to see if there was any more CCTV footage from shops, bars or restaurants in the area. With the little information she had, this was the best plan she could come up with until Markus got back to her. Hopefully he would have good news for her. She eventually found a shop with a camera that could potentially help her search and she decided to use the same car break-in excuse she had used yesterday. The elderly owner of the second-hand bookshop did not think anything strange of it, making it clear the police had not been there yet.

"Pause the screen. There. That's them, the bastards!" she shouted, full of excitement. Realising how loud she had been she quickly added, "Sorry. I'm just happy there's some clear footage of them."

"I thought you were looking for footage of your car getting broken into," the old man said with a confused look on his face.

"These are the people that broke into my car. The footage from the tobacconist where my car was parked wasn't very clear but I was able to see them get into this van and drive into this street. Could I take a copy of this to take to the police?" Cas backpedalled, trying to come across like the housewife she was supposed to be.

The footage was clear enough that she could see the letters and numbers of the licence plate. All Cas could make out through the windshield were the tattooed forearms of the man that she had seen meet Jordan and the woman on the previous footage. Jordan and the woman must be in the back of the van. The driver kept looking to his left and right shiftily, and it didn't seem like it was because he was overly concerned about road safety. If only she had ICU's tech support right now. They would be able to hack into the police systems and find out more about who owned the vehicle. Even if she went to the police with all the information she had gathered, they would just take over and leave her out of the investigation. They would take too long. She knew the key to finding a missing person was speed. Letting someone else continue the investigation was not an option. She felt like she owed it to Jordan and Carrie to finish what she had started. Whenever Cas started a mission, she knew one of her weaknesses was getting attached. Now that she had started this, she would do whatever she could to find the young girl.

She came up with a plan that most people would think was crazy. Crazy enough to work. Markus had told her once: 'no risk, no reward'. She knew he would not agree with it in this case but repeating those words inside her head made her feel like she was doing the right thing, whether she was right or not. This could go wrong in so many ways. Normally it would take weeks to prepare for a mission like this, and usually she had the security of having an entire secret agency behind her as back-up. Right now, she was all alone.

She was going to blow something up in front of the police station. Hopefully this would be a big enough distraction for them to come out and for her to get in, unseen. She began to doubt her plan and her own sanity when she drove past the police station. Three police cars were parked outside, which meant that at least a dozen officers were inside. Would her little explosion be enough to draw them all out? She parked her car a couple of streets away. She planned to escape on public transport, she could not risk having anyone see her get back in her car after the explosion. It would lead them straight back to her house and would quite literally blow up the mission she was actually here for.

Shades and baseball cap on. Hood up. It made her smile that she looked exactly like the woman she was hunting. They say the best way to catch a criminal is to get inside their mind. Every time Cas felt really nervous about something the vein beside her left eye would pulse and it was definitely throbbing now. She walked down the street and chose her targets. One bin just around the corner of the police station, out of sight but close enough to be heard from within the station. Another a little bit further way, she had to keep them busy long enough after all. Most importantly, there were no CCTV cameras anywhere near the bins. Her heart was racing faster than ever before. She was scared. No Markus, no back-up. Just her and her crazy, stupid idea.

"I must be fucking crazy," she muttered as she dropped her second package. Ninety seconds. "One and two and three and four…" Even though she was wearing a watch, she was counting along just in case.

BOOM.

The noise was so loud it gave Cas a fright even though she was expecting it. The bang was followed by two seconds of silence, then a flurry of activity. There was shouting and people running in panic, though she had been careful to pick locations where no one would get hurt. So far, so good.

Several police officers were rushing out of the station after noticing the commotion on the street.

BOOM.

There was the second one. She counted nine officers leaving the building. She ran inside.

"Help! There's a riot! They're beating up the other officers!" She screamed hysterically after she noticed the officer at the front desk not moving. It worked. He sprinted outside to help. She had to be fast. She knew that at least some of them would be back within minutes.

She was using a system the ICU tech team had designed for the White House: a program that installs a hidden untraceable system, giving the user access to the computers on that particular network. It cleverly hides itself in the least-used folders on the computer and the file names automatically change to fit in with existing folders, ensuring the new software goes unnoticed. All contained in a memory stick. The original plan was for Markus to use this system in the White House to gain access to the President's schedule after completing his training. Cas figured she needed it more right now. Besides, a test run wouldn't harm anyone.

Done.

She made her way stealthily out of the building. She was surprised none of the police officers had returned.

Installing the program had definitely taken at least a couple of minutes. She had been ready to lie her way out of her position behind the front desk but it did not seem like she would need to. As she walked along the road, several fire engines and ambulances passed her with wailing sirens. She was starting to feel bad about the disruption she had caused, but then quickly told herself that it was to save a little girl's life and no one had been hurt. "One might have been enough though…" she mumbled when seeing the number of emergency services gathered for the two bin explosions. The type of explosives she had used were just strong enough to create a ton of noise, but they were not strong enough to actually harm anyone – not unless someone had put their head into the bin the moment the bombs had detonated.

Her insane plan had worked. She had made it in and out of the police station unseen. After a meandering journey away from the scene just in case, she slammed the door and sprinted up the stairs of her house. Now all she had to do was see if the device had worked its magic.

17

Another dead end. Cassandra was not surprised that both the car and the registration plates came up as stolen. The van had been reported stolen four days before on the outskirts of Philadelphia. She researched the details and pulled up a picture of the location of where the van had been last seen. The plates belonged to a sixteen year old Mercedes in Baltimore. Even though this felt initially like a defeat, the locations of the theft gave Cas new destinations to continue her search. It was a slim hope, but it was still a lead. She had hoped that these people were stupid enough to use their own vehicle, especially seeing as they had made the mistake of getting caught on camera several times. Their recklessness made Cassandra feel like she had a good chance of catching them and finding Jordan. If they still had her, that is.

Within an hour of finding out the locations Cas had

packed her bags, ready to make a quick impromptu road-trip, northbound. Before all her time had been taken up by ICU, she had always enjoyed travelling alone. Obviously, this was not one of her leisurely trips abroad, but it was just as exciting.

She decided not telling Markus what she was up to was the best approach for the time being. She was going to tell him her plan once she was already on her way. She knew that he would definitely slow her down by trying to talk her out of it if he got the chance. *'Remember what you're here for, Cas,'* or *'This is not your responsibility, Cassandra.'* It irritated her endlessly, the way he always put her name at the end of sentence when he was trying to sound serious or convincing. Sometimes it almost felt like he was using her name as an insult. Her standard response when he did this was to state the fact that she was not a child, which likely made her sound like a petulant teenager. Cassandra ran through the conversation they would have in her head just to silence that little voice inside. That voice was making her doubt whether it was right to tell him now or later. No, later. She was driving to Philadelphia no matter what. Best not be slowed down. For Jordan's sake.

*

Even though she was sure she was doing the right thing, Cas felt the lack of back-up keenly now that she was on the road alone. No Markus, no ICU, no one to tell her what to do but it also meant that there was no one to help her prepare or make a plan. She decided that the best thing would be to retrace the steps since the theft of the van in Philadelphia. As it was the first trace the kidnappers had left behind, it seemed most logical to start there. She hoped that one of the kidnappers had been just as reckless when stealing the van or licence plates. She knew the chances were small. It was wishful thinking to expect a criminal hard enough to abduct a child would do so without a plan. Hopefully the odds would be on her side.

Cassandra started to suspect that luck was *not* on her side after all when the skies began to pelt hailstones as big as table tennis balls half an hour after she set out. Her first American adventure. She had never seen or heard anything like it. The arrhythmic noise the little stones made on the roof of the car sounded like shots fired by a malfunctioning machine gun. It made her nervous. Cas was a confident driver, even in rain and snow, but the noise the aluminium car roof was making triggered something inside her that made her anxious. It was a feeling she had not felt in years whilst driving. She turned up the radio until the speakers started crackling. Anything was better than the noise of frozen bullets right above her head, even Justin Timberlake's 'Mirrors' played loudly enough to cause hearing loss was an improvement.

*

After driving through the torrential rain and hail for over two hours, the skies cleared up just in time for Cas to arrive in Philly. Here, she would trace where the van had been stolen.

After some driving through the streets of town, she suddenly stopped when she saw a place that looked familiar. It was the vacant parking lot across from an old unused factory that she recognised from her photo. There were no cameras, no shops nearby and no possible witnesses. The scene could have come straight out of a movie. The parking lot had the feel of an abandoned set, last used for some controversial clown horror movie. She definitely had to do a background check on the owner of the vehicle after seeing this. Who in their right mind would leave their car here? It was the perfect place to steal a car – the chances of being disturbed or seen here were very small. Perhaps they had only reported the car stolen to draw attention away from themselves. She had to check all possible leads. Eventually one of them would lead her to Jordan. Hopefully.

Exhausted from her first lengthy drive on an American highway Cas decided to find a café nearby to get some food, rest, and contact Markus. It was time to fill him in on her plan. She found a decent looking café not far from the factory. It was busy, which hopefully meant that their coffee was as good as it looked on the billboard picture she had seen when driving into the parking lot. She needed a good cuppa. Every time she had passed one of those 'Tiredness can Kill' signs on the highway, she felt inclined to stop. Driving always made her tired, no matter how rested she was.

Since Markus's training had properly begun, getting in touch had been near impossible. His days were filled with activities from dawn until dusk. Phones were not allowed throughout the day, so the only time they got the chance to speak to each other was before going to bed or the brief moments he had while freshening up after physical exercises. The main way they had been communicating over the last couple of weeks was via text. Telling her partner over text that she was travelling all over the country to find her new friend's missing child was harder than expected, especially since she was really supposed to be only a couple of miles away as his back-up. She was having trouble putting it into words in a way that was short enough to be a text but still long enough to make him understand. That was the hard part. Telling him she was doing some investigating around the corner from their house had been a lot easier. She knew that he would find it hard to get his head around the fact that she was defying direct orders. They had both been told not to leave Washington, DC at this point in the mission, at least not without informing AJ. For a second she questioned her own sanity. Was this little side mission an insane mistake?

After typing and retyping the message differently a dozen times she decided a voice message would be better to get her point of view across properly. She started from the beginning, telling him exactly step by step what had happened and what she had found out so far. Surely he would be able to understand if she told him every little detail. That way he would put himself in her shoes.

Her plan was to downplay this road trip and make it seem like the purpose of her message was to see if he had a response from his friend Barry. Trying to sound surprised that she had not heard from him about the footage, she ended the message. As soon as she hung up, she knew that he would see right through her distraction tactics. She had reiterated that Jordan's safety had depended on it one too many times. He did not know Jordan and he knew that she did not really either. At least not well. After her voicemail, she sent him all the other evidence she had collected yesterday and this morning. Once he got his head around the fact that she was doing this no matter what, he would hopefully be willing to help. As it was only early in the afternoon, chances were that he would not get back to her for hours, especially given that it was a six-minute long voice message. He likely would not even get six minutes to listen to the message properly until the end of his day. At least she had kept one of her promises: she was keeping him up to date on everything she was doing. Sort of. As long as telling him after she had already done it counted…

Cas was starting to feel a little directionless. No new evidence, no one to speak to for advice about what to do next. What if her next stop in Baltimore was just as useless? Was there even any point in continuing this search without any concrete leads? She had to trust her own instincts. She knew that Markus would declare her insane if they spoke, at least to begin with. It would be worth it though, he would know what to do next. Markus was brilliant at coming up with back-up plans whenever they were stuck. She thought about giving up and going home to where she was meant to be. But then Markus popped into her head again, this time saying, "You can find anything on the internet these days." She could see his proud face in front of her waving his smart phone from right to left after finding a critical link for their mission in Uzbekistan. Just before they were due to blindly break into a weapons dealer's house, Markus had found pictures of the dealer partying in his own house on social media. As innocent as they seemed, those photos had helped them to form an image of what the house looked like and, more importantly, where they could hide and find cover. Fifty-year-old blueprints were not necessarily a reliable resource to help prepare for a tactical kill mission. In that fifty years, any number of alterations could have been made, especially to a wealthy arms merchant's house. Blueprints and a photo of the dealer was all ICU had given them. Since that mission, researching a target's social media had become part of their standard mission prep.

Cas ended up spending hours in the café drinking one mocha after another. The caffeine kept her going. She researched every little bit of evidence she had discovered as thoroughly as possible. Even Jordan's principal and teachers got background checks. Carrie and the grandmother were up next. It seemed logical to check out all of Carrie and the deceased husband's families. In a great deal of abduction or kidnapping cases, a family member is often involved in some way or another. The information that Cas could find about Jordan's family came back clean, however. Except for what she found out about Carrie and Michael.

Her new friend had lied to her. Michael had indeed passed away four years ago but not in active duty as a marine as Carrie had claimed. He had been a marine until 2002 when he was dishonourably discharged for drug offences. He fell into addiction. Between his discharge and his death, he had been arrested for theft and other petty crimes several times. The cause of his eventual death was an overdose. But that was not all: besides lying about her husband, it turned out that her new friend also had a record. Her little stealth program on the police station computers let her see that Carrie had racked up numerous warnings and three arrests, all for stealing.

Cassandra was shocked, her new friend was not as sweet and innocent as she made out to be. She was a bit taken aback by this new information about her friend's past but she realised this was not important. Maybe Carrie had been the reason for her embarking on this manhunt at first but that was before she knew something was really wrong. It had seemed like the right thing to do to help her new friend. But once Cas saw the footage of little Jordan being led away, she knew this was serious. She was doing this for her now.

For a moment Cas was stunned that Carrie had slipped past her radar so easily. Usually her instincts about people were spot-on, but Carrie had seemed like a sweet suburban mother, as straight-laced and ordinary as they come. According to her file, Jordan had been in foster care for six months after Michael died because Carrie had not been able to cope. She had been in rehab. Her husband had left this earth but unfortunately had left his drug habit behind. The last thing Cas would have expected was for Carrie to be an ex-addict. Carrie was always dressed in nice expensive clothes and was so well put together. Cas was frustrated that she had felt so close to her and Carrie had hidden all this from her. She reminded herself that the mother's past was not the daughter's fault and it was Jordan's safety that was paramount.

After what felt like another million dead ends, Cas finally found something. It was small, maybe insignificant, but it was something. The name of the person reporting the stolen licence plates did not match the name of the person who they belonged to. Why would you report the theft of licence plates that were not your own? Maybe it had been a witness. If they witnessed the theft, maybe they witnessed something else as well. This person could be the key to uncovering the identity of the kidnappers.

The woman who had reported the theft was an old lady living near the owner of the plates, which meant that her theory could be correct. Her optimism turned into a burst of energy. She at least had somewhere to go now. A lead, however small, felt like a breakthrough after searching the web and police records in a dingy overcrowded café for hours.

If Markus had been there with her, he would have pulled her back to the ground and told her it was just a small lead which was potentially useless. It was sometimes hard to keep Cas on the ground with both feet. She was a dreamer – in another life she could have been a total hippie, a free spirit. Any small lead could give her the feeling that she had just found the solution to everything. Markus was miles away though, so she kept on dreaming.

*

By the time she got to Baltimore it was too late to knock on Ms Susan O'Connor's door. She would have to wait until morning. Patience, however, was not one of her strengths.

Cas parked her SUV in front of the first motel she could find. She felt lucky that she was able to find a bed for the night so easily. It would not have been so easy in Europe, not without having to drive into a town or city. Sketchy was the only word that came to mind after swiping the key card and opening the door to the funky smelling room. She had learned the word from Carrie. It made her ruefully chuckle at the fact that she had learned the word from someone who had seemed so far from its definition but who had more than her fair-share of sketchiness in her past.

18

Thankfully the first impression she was given by the odour of the room did not match the quality of the bed. Cas had not slept this well since moving to the States. The bed was perfect: thick, firm pillows on top of a super soft mattress, so soft Cas felt like she was floating. Being so incredibly comfortable made Cas change her plans, even though Cas was not usually one for straying from her schedule. She normally liked to stick to whatever she had noted down in the diary in her head. Instead of getting up as early as was acceptable to knock on Ms O'Connor's door, she decided to sink down and doze some more until she had to get ready and check out.

Cas was dreaming about buying a bed exactly like this one when she suddenly realised the sound she was hearing was the room next to her being vacuumed. The horrible sound of a vacuum cleaner on tiles being pushed against the wall repeatedly could wake anyone up. She checked the time on her phone and immediately jumped out of bed. It was ten past eleven, ten minutes after her check out time. This usually never happened to Cassandra, early mornings were her thing. 'We can sleep when we're dead,' was what she always told Markus whenever she was tasked with waking him at the break of dawn.

Ten minutes later Cas was at the reception desk handing in her key card. She normally did not shower at night but had done so before going to bed last night. It was almost like her mind knew she would not have time for one in the morning. It made her feel like things happened for a reason, but if that was the case, how had she got herself involved in this crazy situation? Was it just to stop her from dying of boredom? Being a housewife was definitely not something that suited Cassandra, even if it was a housewife who was also a spy. She needed action in her life – adrenaline, and lots of it.

After grabbing a quick coffee, Cas was standing on the doorstep of her newest lead. "Hi there, are you Ms O'Connor?"

"Depends who's asking."

"My name is Natasha Connelly. I work as an investigator for the DC Missing Persons Department. May I come in and ask you a couple of questions?" Cas said as she held up a police badge. The badge had been part of the ICU mission kit, along with FBI credentials, explosives, the memory stick, and a Glock 22 – all just in case they were needed. "You reported your neighbour's licence plates stolen last week, is that right?"

"Johnny lives a couple of houses down the street. You can see the house from here, it's the one with the wooden porch and hanging chair…Would you like a cup of coffee or tea?" the old lady asked as she moved into the house, gesturing for Cas to follow.

"I'm okay, thank you. So why was it yourself that reported the plates stolen and not Johnny?" she asked Ms O'Connor.

"I knew that Johnny and Alice – his girlfriend – were away to see family in Ontario all week. When I saw this woman walking towards their door, I couldn't help being nosey. I watched her ring the bell and at first I guessed she was selling something or asking for directions, but then she walked to the window at the side of the house and had a good look inside. Pretty suspicious if you ask me."

"What did the woman do then?"

"I thought she might be trying to break in but then she walked over to the car parked on the drive and started unscrewing the plates. That's when I went to call the police but of course she was long gone by the time they got here. Someone terrorising our neighbourhood was clearly not important enough to the police."

Ms O'Connor reminded Cassandra of the old lady that had lived next to her parents' house when she was growing up. That lady, just like this one, was obviously a little lonely and enjoyed having some company. Whenever Cas used to go over to bring her neighbour some food or groceries she would not stop talking until you cut her off, often leaving you feeling rude and insensitive. Cas got the feeling that Ms O'Connor was capable of the same thing if she got the chance, so she decided it would be best to steer the conversation and keep the reigns in hand. At least that way she would avoid feeling like a rude bitch when it was time to go.

"The reason I'm here is because Johnny's licence plates were found on a car used in the kidnapping of a young girl in Washington, DC. The woman you saw stealing the plates is probably involved somehow. I'd like to ask you to take a minute and have a good think about what she looked like, what she was wearing and which way she went. Did she get into a car? Anything you can remember could help us save this little girl."

The old lady was shocked, this kind of thing only happened on television. After a moment of silence, the old lady got up and started to pace.

"She had very dark brown hair, longer than yours and straight. I think she had a fringe but I'm not sure. She sort of looked like that actress, the one with all the orphans?" She had begun circling her dining table and seemed agitated in her efforts to remember.

Cas quickly grabbed her phone and did a quick image search. "Is this the actress you mean?" Cas asked, holding up a photo of Angelina Jolie.

"Yes, that one right there. She looked just like her, maybe not as striking and with slightly broader hips," she said whilst pointing at a picture of Jolie in the movie *Salt*. "I think she was wearing a cap and her clothes were mostly dark. She had a rucksack because that's what she put the licence plates in…After that I went to call the police and stopped paying attention to her, so I'm not sure how or which way she left."

Cas thanked Ms O'Connor and took her leave. Once she was back in the car, she started thinking about all she had discovered over the past few days. She knew what Jordan's kidnappers looked like, at least the woman that had convinced her to leave the school with her. She knew that the woman's accomplice had his arms covered in tattoos and she knew what direction they had come from. How far had they travelled to steal the van? Why had they travelled so far to kidnap Jordan? Was she targeted specifically or had they just seen an opportunity? What did a middle-aged Angelina Jolie lookalike want with the girl? All these questions were making Cassandra's head spin until her thoughts were interrupted by the sound of her phone ringing. It was Markus. Finally.

"Markus, your timing could not be better. How are you?"

"No, this isn't about me. I listened to your message. What the hell are you doing in Philadelphia?! If ICU finds out what you're up to, you'll be on the first flight back to Amsterdam. The day before yesterday you said you were just helping your friend search for her daughter in DC. I thought this was a case of a spoilt runaway looking to scare her mother for a few hours when I told you to go ahead. I've done some digging myself since I listened to your voicemail. Do you even know what you've got involved with?"

Cas could tell that Markus was pissed off and wanted to bite her head off but his tone was surprisingly not as angry as she expected. He probably didn't have the energy to properly rip into her.

"I'm in Baltimore now…" she started off as slow and measured as possible. "The licence plates used during the kidnapping were stolen here…I've come so far, I can't give up now, Markus. I know I can do a better job than the police. I have a feeling something horrible has happened to Jordan. I can't just give up on her. Not now. Markus, you know me, you know my instincts are usually right. I have to finish this…I do wish you were here though, that would definitely make things easier."

"Me too. At least then I wouldn't have to worry about you while I'm being shouted at by my drill sergeant. I do have some info for you but please promise me you'll be careful. These people are serious criminals if the intel I have is right."

"I promise. Of course I know to be careful, these are criminals who've kidnapped a little girl!" Cas said with a slightly offended tone. "Did you hear back from Barry?"

"Yes, I did. Sending you the file as we speak. You said the only thing you could make out with the male accomplice from the footage you sent me was that his arms were covered in tattoos. I had a look and one of the tattoos looked strangely familiar. Remember I told you about the odd journey I had on the plane when I was first flying to the States? Well, that angry and threatening man travelling with the young girl on my flight had a lot of tattoos on his arms too. I remember one of them looked a lot like one on your mystery man. The guy was arrested and processed after the plane landed. I got Barry to do a check on him and the tattoo in general. It's definitely the same tattoo. According to Barry, they're both part of the K&A Gang. Members of the K&A have been arrested for drug trafficking, assault, extortion and even murder. I guess we can add human trafficking to that list since that flight." He let all that information sink in for a bit. "I wish you weren't doing this by yourself, Cas," he said almost mournfully.

"You could go rogue and come help me," she said in all seriousness.

"Very funny. You know I can't do that. Promise me you'll give me updates on any new locations you go to. *Before* you go to them. The file includes the previous arrest records and addresses of all the known gang members. I have to go now...but be careful, Cassandra. I love you."

"I will. Thank you," Cas said quickly, surprised at the 'I love you' she had not seen coming. Since Markus had started his training, their conversations had been so short there had been barely any time for speaking about their personal lives and what was going on between them. As soon as she put the phone down, Cas felt silly for not saying it back. She knew she had possibly caused some disappointment on the other side of the line.

19

Even though Cassandra had gone to bed late after sitting up going through arrest records half the night, she woke up feeling refreshed. She had gone back to the motel she had stayed in the night before and slept in the world's comfiest bed again. She felt a little guilty about her second lie-in in as many days, especially since a little girl's life was at stake, but she figured that the gang members were unlikely to get up so early anyway. At least she was now well-rested and she finally had a plan to find Jordan.

The toughest part this morning was to choose where to go first. She had gone from barely having any ideas to having potential leads spread out over two states. Her plan was to follow the leads closest to Philadelphia first. Neither of the two had shown up in Markus's file but she was going to try to pin down some of the other gang members to spill more information about her Angelina Jolie lookalike, a name or address if she was lucky. She figured it would be easier to question them about her than someone she could only describe as a chubby tattooed man.

Her first stop was a mechanic working just outside of central Philadelphia named Antonin Dwozonek. According to his file, he had been part of the gang since the very start so there was a good chance that he would know the mystery woman. He had been arrested earlier in the year for stabbing a member of a rival gang. If the file was to be believed, the other party had instigated the fight, which was why Dwozonek had received a relatively short sentence and had been out on parole after serving only a small part of his sentence. He now worked in a small garage on the outskirts of the city. The other reason Dwozonek had stood out was his known address was only five blocks away from where the van had been stolen. At least he would be relatively easy to track down as his parole was for another four months and it was one of the conditions of him being out that he hold the job until that time. Now all Cas had to do was find a way to get the information she wanted without causing any suspicion.

"Are you Antonin Dwozonek?"

"Depends who's asking," the skinny man spat out whilst looking her up and down with a sneer on his face. It made her laugh inwardly that his words were the same as those of Ms O'Connor's the day before but the two attitudes could not have been more different.

"I am Special Agent Connelly with the FBI. Mrs Heiser, your parole officer, told me where I could find you."

"Ugh, that bitch. She's been making my life a living hell for months now. What the hell do you want?"

Bringing up the parole officer was obviously not a great idea. Dwozonek sounded bitter and was probably more reluctant now to help Cas, but at least he didn't seem to be questioning who she was.

"I know that you know this woman," Cas said whilst holding up an enlarged screenshot of the Angelina Jolie lookalike. "I need to know where she is. Tell me that and I'll be out of your hair. I might even make it worth your while," she said while reaching for her wallet. She could see a flicker of interest in his eyes and wondered how close he was to tipping his hand. Money or loyalty. She had seen the tracks and bruises on his arms, she knew he was a man who was used to giving in to temptation. Some other thought must have passed through his head, however, and he looked Cas straight in the eye.

"I've never seen the broad."

Cas simply continued looking at him. For a moment they were both silent.

Dwozonek gave in first and broke the stalemate, "Is that all? 'Cuz if it is, FUCK OFF." He grabbed one of his tools and slid back under the car he had been working on.

Goodbye to you too, Cassandra thought as she walked out of the garage. She was smiling as if he had just given her the kidnapper's location. As soon as she had realised that exercising her authority was not the way to go with Antonin, she had jumped to plan B. Offering him money was a long shot, she didn't really expect him to go for it,

143

but she did want to make him feel uncomfortable. If he even considered the deal for a moment, he would now be all the more eager to atone for his almost-disloyalty. Either way, the fact that a FBI agent was seemingly crooked enough to offer a bribe to a known gang member should tip him off that something was up. She wasn't likely to be so intent on finding Jolie 2.0 for a spot of lunch. He would be nervous – nervous enough to contact Jolie to warn her.

Cassandra jumped into her SUV and grabbed her binoculars out of the glove compartment.

"Bingo," she said with satisfaction, as if she had the final number for a full card. As soon as he thought that she was out of sight, Dwozonek had crawled out from under the car and immediately made a phone call. All she had to do now was find out what number Dwozonek had dialled. Before he had finished his call she had already typed his home address from his arrest record into the navigation system. She had no time to spare. After seeing this guy, she knew enough of the K&A now to know that Jordan's wellbeing would depend on every single minute.

*

After a twelve-minute drive Cas parked her car outside a rundown block of apartments. They were old, dark and dirty – exactly what she had expected. She sprinted up the stairs on the outside of the building. If saving Jordan had not already been enough to motivate Cas to run, the smell certainly would have. Even though she was outdoors, the smell of urine and vomit was pungent. And of course Dwozonek's apartment was on the top floor. Out of breath, she walked along the balcony to door 7c. *Damn it.* The door had an extra lock. It was an old-fashioned affair, sturdy and built to last. There was no way she was going to break that lock. She sighed and moved to the front window. She hoped none of Dwozonek's neighbours would hear or care what was going on.

Cas started smashing in the window with the butt of her pistol. It was more of a viewing pane than a proper window, as tall as the door but only just over a foot wide. She had to knock all the glass out of the frame to fit through without cutting herself. After every further smash, she looked around to see if anyone had come out to check what the noise was about. Cas felt nervous. Knocking the glass out with her gun took a lot longer than anticipated. Still no sign of any curious neighbours, though. *They must be used to it here,* Cas muttered as she climbed in through the broken window. Kensington was one of the roughest and poorest areas in the city. The only Kensington Cas had ever been to before was the borough of Kensington in London – definitely a contrast to this place.

The flat itself was also unsurprising. It stank of booze, dirty socks and a bin that was in dire need of being emptied. The decided lack of furniture was not going to win Dwozonek any design awards, but it made Cas's search for a phone bill amidst the rubbish slightly easier. A giant pile of bills and letters sat on a shelf in the hallway. All unopened, of course. She rifled through the pile until she came across an envelope from PureTalk. She tucked this into her jacket and decided to search the rest of the apartment just in case. The living room was small and dark – old sheets and blankets were pinned up over the windows to keep out the light. The only glass that wasn't covered was the door leading to the balcony at the back of the building. A big leather sofa took up half the room. A TV unit and DVD player, but no TV. Her guess was that he had pawned it to cover his debts. The bedroom was just as empty: a single stained mattress lay on the floor. No bedding, as it seemed he had used all of it to block out the light. The only other thing in the room was a cupboard with some clothes in it.

Just when Cassandra decided that there was no point in continuing searching this empty home, she heard police sirens outside. She ran to the front of the flat and peeked out to see whether they were stopping here. *FUCK!* She saw two officers get out of their car. Someone must have called the police. She had gotten too comfortable after not seeing anyone respond to the noise she had been making. *Fuck.* There was only one staircase. She could pretend to live here and simply walk down the stairwell, but she was screwed if whoever had called the police had gotten a good look at her. She was stuck.

20

She had thought about her options for too long. She had no choice now but to use the balcony out the back as her escape route. She was furious with herself: first for letting her guard down and taking too long at the apartment, and secondly for failing to make her escape plan in time. Now she had no choice. How often was she going to let her doubts get in the way before learning she had to act immediately, at least in situations like this one. One day overthinking would be her downfall – she just hoped it wouldn't be today.

On her way to the back of the flat, she pulled over the shelves in the hallway in an attempt to slow them down. She made her way to the balcony and cursed that Antonin Dwozonek lived on the top floor a second time. Cas had never been afraid of heights but climbing down from a seventh floor apartment did make her a little nervous.

The balconies of each apartment were about two meters apart. Her plan was to jump down diagonally until she made it to the bottom. She took a deep breath and used the chair out on the balcony to climb on top of the balcony wall. She leapt down and just as she reached the balcony on the floor below, she heard two voices shouting at her.

"Police! Stop right there!"

She didn't stop to look but a glimpse told her at least one of them had a gun pointed on her. She ran across the balcony as fast as she could and jumped the next wall, flying across it like Spiderman or a parkour expert. Her landing was not so graceful, though. The clotheshorse on the balcony got her tangled up, leaving her with a cut on her arm and what felt like a twisted ankle. *Thank God,* she thought when she saw that this apartment's balcony door was open. There was no way she could have done another jump, not with her ankle already starting to throb.

The apartment was filled with people: several adults and children, some sitting at the little round dining table, the rest squeezed onto the couch. An older lady was walking out of the kitchen. As soon as she looked up and noticed Cas, she screamed. Cas managed to get out a quick, "Sorry!" before dashing across the room. No one else had time to react. The commotion did not start until she managed to reach the front door and pulled it open. Like a hunted deer, she raced down the stairs as fast as she could, limping all the while. The officers had had to circle the building to find her but they were not far behind.

As she jumped into her car she could see them bounding down the stairs in pursuit.

Her Cherokee's tires squealed as she careened out of the car park. Only seconds later, the blare of police car sirens wailed through the air. The police car was a few hundred yards away now, but Cas knew that she was in trouble. She idly wondered how long it would take ICU to find out what she had been up to over the past few days. When she noticed the cops getting closer she put her foot down on the gas pedal as hard as she could, zigzagging through the narrow streets of Kensington. Her hands were shaking and clammy, making her grip on the steering wheel precarious. All she could do was hope that no one ended up underneath her car. Every time she saw a moving object – she didn't care whether it was a car, human or dog – she beeped as loud, long and erratically as she could to make them get out of her way. She could see the flashing blue lights in her windshield mirror but at least she had created some distance. The knowledge that she would have been able to lose them, no bother, if this had been Amsterdam, Berlin or London frustrated her to no end. She had no idea where she was heading and putting on the navigation system would have taken her eyes off the road. She was driving too fast to risk that.

When she reached a main road and saw no police cars in sight, she allowed herself a moment to breathe. For a split second she enjoyed the adrenaline of it all. Then it dawned on her that this was definitely the end of her career.

How could I have been so reckless? Who in their right mind would smash a window in full view of anyone who might have been passing on the street below or in the flats across? She could have used her phony FBI credentials to get into the neighbour's apartment and got in to Dwozonek's that way. "You fucking idiot!" she cursed at herself. She hit the steering wheel in anger. Maybe she didn't need to learn to make decisions more quickly, she certainly acted on them quickly just now. Too bad they were stupid decisions.

Cassandra was still driving fast, less erratically now, but she needed to keep the distance between her and the police. Her anger at herself was interrupted by her phone ringing: AJ. She was not sure if picking up was the smartest plan. He would, no doubt, be furious and the last thing she needed right now was to be distracted.

"Cassandra, what the hell is going on? Why are you not in DC? The plug on your mission hasn't been pulled yet," AJ's angry voice shouted at her through the surround sound system of the car. His face then appeared on the screen of her navigation system. Apparently not picking up his call was not an option, at least not when it was AJ who had the resources to hack into any device.

"AJ…I can't explain what's going on just now. I'm sort of in the middle of something…I'll explain everything later," she tried to sound as calm as possible.

"Cassandra, I know you're being chased by the police. I have eyes and ears everywhere. That's how I know you're in Philadelphia. What the hell, Cassandra? I knew sending you as Markus's handler was a bad idea.

You're the one that needs a handler!" He took a breath and tried to calm down. "The police have called for back-up and helicopter assistance. You need to dump the car. I'm going to guide you out of the shit you've got yourself into. Put your headset on and listen…You better have a damn good reason for all this," AJ growled out, more pissed off than she had ever heard him.

"Yes, AJ," was all Cassandra said. She knew she had royally fucked up. Her plan to solve Jordan's kidnapping unnoticed had failed.

"You need to take a right and then a sharp left. I'm guiding you to the Market-Frankford Line. We'll need to get the timing and distance between you and the police cars right so you can jump onto a carriage as the train departs. Where is Markus?"

"At the training centre. Where else would he be? And what did you mean by, 'the plug has not been pulled *yet*'? I had no idea that was even close to happening."

"Take a right. Do you even read the emails I send you? Or watch the news? There's talk that the President will be impeached within the next twenty-four hours. They've found evidence that he offered bribes to his main opponent to throw the election. Apparently, he's also been helping his son-in-law evade taxes since he's been in power… Third exit up ahead. Take the first left. Okay, stop here. Leave the car in this alleyway. Run to the end and you'll see the entrance to the station."

Cassandra blindly followed what AJ's voice told her, having now picked up his call on her phone.

Her whole body felt cold with sweat.

"The train on platform two departs in ninety seconds. The closest police car is less than a quarter mile behind you. I've got you on CCTV now, Cas. When you come out of the alley, walk to the right before you cross to the station. The second shop you pass has scarves on display hanging outside. Grab one. The only description they have of you just now is your hair and leather jacket. Get rid of your jacket. Good. That's the police just reached your car. Cross the road towards the main entrance. They won't be able to follow you there <u>as they are</u>. Call me again as soon as you find somewhere quiet."

*

By herself again, without even AJ's stern voice telling her what to do, Cas sat on the train and rubbed her temple in stress. Even though she had just escaped a police chase she knew that the real stress had yet to even begin. ICU now knew that she had not been playing according to the rules. Whether the President was impeached or not, she was going home – that much was certain. As soon as she got off the train, she tried to call Markus.

No answer. She sighed. Cassandra had always been a star at lying herself out of tricky situations but she could not seem to come up with a believable story this time, She was going to tell AJ the truth, all of it. There was no way she could lie herself out of this one.

She looked across the compartment and watched a

mother and daughter about Jordan's age laugh and talk to one another. The love between the two was obvious. That's what Jordan deserved too. The image of the two in front of her helped her make up her mind. Forget the consequences – she needed to finish this. Her ICU career was over no matter what. At least if she found Jordan, it all would have been worth something. If she wasn't already too late…

21

Telling the truth worked out a million times better than Cassandra had ever expected. After the insane police chase, she had taken extra care in finding somewhere quiet and private and had settled on a small seedy motel. The fact that AJ had not immediately called back surprised her but he probably knew that she needed some time to collect her thoughts. It seems her honesty in telling the state of matters from start to end convinced him to not send a grab team to pick her up. There was a human side to AJ after all, though she'd never seen it before. He was going to keep what he knew under the radar for now and let her finish what she had started. At first she had to double check if what she heard him saying was correct, it had seemed so unlike him.

"You're very lucky your actual mission is about to be cancelled. It's the only reason I'm letting you go through with this nonsense, Cassandra, but there will be consequences once this is over," he warned her before hanging up. His entire reaction to the situation still surprised her. AJ had never seemed like the type that would be okay with adhering to the rules by anything less than one hundred percent. He had always been a bit of robot – she hadn't even been sure if he was capable of emotions or making compromises before now. Being wrong had never felt so good.

After extracting a promise that Cassandra would never disclose his role in any of this, he agreed to help her. Of course she would never tell a soul, it was her ass on the line. Within minutes he found out the locations of the last three people Antonin Dwozonek had called. If he had been helping Cas from the start she would have likely found Jordan days earlier. When it came to computers and remotely hacking into systems, AJ was a certifiable genius.

One of the locations was an overseas address but the other two were reasonably close. One was an address in the western part of Philadelphia, the other was a forty-five minute drive east. One of these had to be where they were keeping Jordan. Dwozonek had made the three calls within a space of twenty minutes. Cas's biggest fear was that her plan to make him nervous had worked too well and that the gang had moved Jordan in a panic. Even worse if they got spooked and decided to make the girl vanish before they could be connected properly to her disappearancc. This was a new worry for Cas: she didn't usually carry so much guilt and such a heavy sense of duty during her missions. Admittedly most of her targets had not been innocent victims and this was a blameless little girl. It was also the first time the responsibility lay solely on her shoulders and the first time she had to do virtually all the planning and thinking herself. She certainly never felt so exposed when she was working with Markus. This one was all on her.

The second address was in Hammonton, New Jersey, likely somewhere a bit more rural. The one actually in Philadelphia would take her just as long to get to. Something inside her told her that she did not have time to get this wrong. If Jordan was still alive, she needed to hurry now that K&A knew someone was on their tail. She decided to call AJ back. He was on her side now, sort of. She could use his advice and expertise. He had been with ICU for years and they dealt with cases like this regularly, though usually only when the local authorities failed to garner any leads. ICU would step in anonymously and tip them off or feed them information.

"Hypothetically speaking, in your experience, would you think it more likely a kidnapped little girl to be held at a rural address or at an urban location…?" Cas queried, in a nod to AJ's insistence that they keep pretending that he didn't know what she was talking about.

"Give me a moment to…think." She could hear him tapping away furiously on the other end. "Hypothetically speaking, *if* the location in the city is an area with mostly one bedroom apartments, well, that would be a less than ideal place to hold an abducted child. If the rural address was, say, in a location like Hammonton, it would be a small farm, particularly a now abandoned farm where the previous owner died seven years ago. Most peculiar that the energy bills seem to be at an all-time high when no one is listed as resident there…"

Cas had missed this sort of back-up, even if everything was couched in ridiculously transparent hypotheticals. Within minutes, AJ had been able to find and relay information that would have taken her days to find on the ground.

*

Now that she had a destination, she needed a ride. Borrowing a vehicle from a civilian would be the fastest solution – adding car theft to her list of transgressions was a minor blip when she was already going to get done for breaking in and running from the police. She would return it afterwards.

On her way into the motel, Cas had seen signs pointing to a car park around the back. It was dark now, the car park was secluded, and the motel was definitely too cheap to have any working cameras in place: perfect. For once she was glad it was not summer yet. The lack of light made jimmying a car door unnoticed a lot easier. After all, there was no need to make Natasha Connelly's record any longer than it had to be…or longer than it already was. The only thing that would make this even easier was the toolkit that was currently sitting in the trunk of her poor abandoned Cherokee. The thin metal no-smoking sign would have to do. She strolled into the parking lot and hoped luck was on her side and that the cars in the lot would match the quality of the motel. She would struggle starting a new car with such basic tools but an old tin can would be a piece of cake. She hoped.

An old Ford caught her eye as soon as she made her way round the corner. Not that she had much to choose from. There was only three cars in the lot and she spotted the red light of an alarm system on one immediately, the other did not look like it would survive the drive out of the car park without falling apart. She approached the Ford and slid her makeshift tool between the door and the window. Her hand slipped on the first go and she froze. A loud blare of an alarm rent the air. *Fuck.* She was sure there was no alarm on the old piece of junk!

Cassandra knelt down to hide herself from view. Her hurt ankle twinged at the sudden movement. She took a moment to breathe, and only then realised that the alarm was not coming from the old Ford at all. She was so focused on what she was doing that it took her a while to pinpoint where the noise was actually coming from. It was a roadside maintenance truck making stops around the corner.

After the initial scare, getting into her new borrowed car was easy. Driving it, however, was another matter. The steering wheel started shaking as soon as the speedometer hit fifty miles an hour. At least being forced to drive well under the speed limit would give her a chance to mentally prepare for whatever was coming. She was determined to find Jordan today, no matter what it took.

The best possible scenario would be if Jordan was at the location healthy and unharmed, but she had been missing for nearly a week and Cassandra knew she had to be more realistic. The worst case scenario would be if the farmhouse was empty and swept of all traces. If she could get her hands on just one of the K&A, she would be able to put her interrogation skills to use. It was certainly not one of her favourite things to do but she was no stranger to having to pull the nails off a target to get them to talk. In a high-stakes situation in Zurich years ago, she had fired at a terrorist's knees to retrieve a code to disarm a bomb in the capital's Hauptbahnhof. The screams he had let out after she shot him had echoed in her head for weeks. He only gave up the code when she threatened to shoot off his testicles next. They had prevented thousands from being hurt, or worse, that day. Cassandra felt a similar weight of responsibility on her now, even though there was only one known victim. There could easily be dozens of other girls in Jordan's position. She was ready to do what she had to in order to ensure their safety. She went over all possible scenarios a hundred times. The drive seemed endless.

*

The navigation system on her phone told her she was five minutes away. This was it – the moment she had been working towards for days. The nerves were

159

starting to kick in. She was about the face the most dangerous gang in Philadelphia. Alone.

It seemed like a strange location for a gang hideout. Even though it was dark and there were no streetlights, she could see from the vast fields on either side of the road that she was in proper farm country. Houses were miles apart. It would be an awfully inconvenient location for regular gang dealings unless they were trying to hide something or someone…

She parked the car a field away from the farm just in case anyone could see the road from the property. She snuck through the sparse woods surrounding the house. She could see a light coming from the farmhouse, which hopefully meant that someone was in. Cas double checked her Glock was loaded. She had left most of her things in the Cherokee but had thankfully remembered to take her knife and her gun before deserting the car. She removed the black-bladed knife she had hidden inside her boot. She knew that the lighter she travelled, the higher the chances she would be able to tiptoe around unnoticed.

Suddenly she remembered the promise she had made. She was going to keep it this time. She sent Markus her location before switching the device to silent mode. All she needed was for him or someone else to message her while she was trying to be unseen. The farmhouse was so remote and it was so silent around her that whoever was in that house would hear a noise like her phone instantly. There was something unnerving about the silence. No birds, no traffic, no sign of life…The only noise she could hear was the soft rustling of the leaves in the breeze but while it usually relaxed her, the sound only made her more anxious. The closer she got to the house, the louder her heartbeat sounded in her head. She decided to make a full circle through the woods to get a good look from all sides.

Three cars were parked beside the barn: two trucks and a Cadillac. She could see a strip of light shining through the bottom of the big barn door. According to AJ, this hadn't been a working farm for seven years. There were definitely no cows in that barn. Cas began to inch closer when she heard voices coming from the house. Two voices. Arguing?

She was not able to hear what they were saying but the way the voices were raised one after the other certainly made it sound like it was a heated discussion. She tried to get closer to hear but by the time she got close enough, a door inside the house slammed. By now, she had made it to the bottom of what appeared to be the kitchen window. She very slowly inched up and peeked through. She was in the right place.

Sitting at the kitchen table with her head buried in her hands sat the very Angelina Jolie lookalike she had been looking for. Even though Cas had only grainy video footage to go on, she was certain that this was the woman who had led Jordan away from her school. She knew it even without seeing her face.

Cas continued walking around the rest of the house. There was no trace of anything unusual in any of the rooms she could see into. She had circled the house entirely with no luck when she came to a small shed attached to the side of the house. As soon as she put her face against the window, she no longer needed to look inside to know what was in there – she could smell it. The shed must have been filled with cannabis plants, and a lot of them at that. No luck there. If Jordan was on this property, she had to be upstairs or in the barn. She decided to try the barn first. She knew the woman was inside the house and would probably hear her if she tried to get in. It was too silent to open a door unnoticed.

She quickly looked to check if the woman was where she had last seen her. Cas was thrilled to see that she had been joined by the co-kidnapper as well. This was her chance. She rushed over to the barn and tried to open the large door as quietly as possible.

Nope. The wheel at the bottom of the slide door made more noise than a screaming baby. There was no way they had not heard the noise from across the yard. She had to be fast.

The barn was lit by a light that seemed to be coming from a large gazebo in the back. *Why was there a gazebo indoors?* The rest of the place looked like a standard shed filled with junk and old appliances. Cas knew that someone would come looking soon after the noise the door had made, so she made her way towards the gazebo with her back turned, keeping an eye on the door and attempting to hide behind objects along the way. Halfway there, she walked into a large tarp-covered object.

The shape of it made her believe it was the van they had stolen. She lifted a corner of the cover just slightly and could see the Maryland registration plate, just as she had expected. She knew the numbers of those plates stolen in Baltimore better than any of her own.

A noise drew her attention away from the car. The man was crossing the yard. She could make out the figure of the tattooed man coming her way. He had not seen her yet but he knew she was there. He seemed unarmed from this distance but she couldn't be sure. She had her gun out ready to take action. She slowly made her way back through the aisles of junk towards the door.

As soon as he was close enough that she had him hemmed in, she stepped out, "Stop. Show me your–"

She heard a crack. The only thing she was aware of was the cold of metal against the back of her head. All the air was forced out of her lungs. There was a ringing in her ears but she could make out nothing else. Everything else was silent – as silent as the night had been before she had ever walked into this trap.

She hit the floor.

22

"Look who's decided to join the party," a male voice drawled.

Cas was confused when she first came to. Her head felt like it was about to explode. Her sight was blurry. Then she realised she must have gotten a blow to her head. She tried to stand up, only to find that she was tied to a rusted pipe with her hands behind her back. She struggled against the ties for a moment, but they were firm. She didn't know where the voice had come from.

She blinked away the film in her eyes and realised exactly where she was. She was tied to the back of the wall of the shed. Now that she could see, she had to squint to block out the blinding floodlights set up in the gazebo. Colours danced before her eyes when she looked away and she had to readjust her eyes again. What she saw made her freeze.

The tent was set up with two rows of stretchers, two rows of three, and on the stretchers lay six undersized bodies. Children. They weren't moving.

She scanned the bodies, desperate for a sign of life. The six little girls all looked nearly identical lying there, until she spotted one in particular. Jordan!

"Jordan! Wake up, hun," she managed to rasp out. She renewed her struggle with the ties behind her back but there was no response. That was when she noticed the subtle rise and fall of one of the girls' chests. They were still alive!

"She can't hear you, Officer Connelly," that same voice announced as a tall, skinny man walked into her view. "It's time for you and I to have a little chat." She saw immediately that the man had the same tattoo as the kidnapper, marking him as another member of the K&A. The only hair on his head was his eyebrows and an oddly shaped beard. His eyes were frighteningly intense even through his dark-rimmed glasses.

"What have you done to them? You may be known criminals, but these are innocent little girls! Have you no scruples? If I were you, I would get out of here. Back-up is on the way."

His thin mouth turned up at one side in a wry smile. "Somehow I doubt that, Natasha, or whoever you are really. I knocked you out about two hours ago. It'd be a bit insulting if they weren't already here by now, don't you think? Secondly, your credentials are fake, bitch. So who are you and what the hell are you doing here?"

"I'm not telling you anything until you tell me what you've done to the girls."

"What I do or don't tell you doesn't matter, sweets. You won't see another sunrise."

In frustration, Cas kicked out and twisted against her constraints.

The man only laughed at her. "Don't bother. The second you manage to break those zip ties is the second I put a bullet in you. Your own bullet, in fact. I've just given the girlies a little cocktail to help them sleep. A lovely bit of temporary paralysis courtesy of Sugammadex with just a touch of ketamine. I created the combo myself."

The psycho actually looked proud of himself. This must have been what she had been drugged with the night someone had broken into her house, the night she thought she was just a victim of a random robbery. Cas suddenly felt a great sense of clarity. Everything was coming together. Her thoughts were crazy, she knew they were, but she needed to know for sure.

"Why did you choose these girls?"

"Nope. You still haven't told me who you are."

"My name is Natasha Connelly. I'm a private detective hired to find Jordan Williams. My turn. Why do the girls all look so alike? What are you going to do to them?"

"One question at a time. There's no rush, we have all night together, darling," he leered at her. The look in his eyes was the evil look of all the criminals she had ever dealt with put together, but worse. The thought of having to spend the entire night talking to this creep made her feel ill. "One of our customers ordered them. He wanted six girls under the age of ten, all to look as similar to each other as possible. A kind of box-set if you will. I don't ask why. As for what he's going to do to them, I'm sure you can probably guess. Might be best if I gave them another shot of my special cocktail before dropping them off…just to ease them into things.

"My turn to ask now. How did you find us?"

"Dwozonek called you two minutes after I spoke to him. I had someone trace the call to this location. Where are they being taken?"

"Fucking useless idiot! He'll definitely get an earful from me. Thank fuck he didn't send the actual police this way, I would have killed him if he had…Saudi Arabia. That's why they're all sleeping so peacefully. They're going in the cargo hold."

"This is sick. He must be paying you a lot to send these innocent girls off like cows to the slaughter. Why Jordan? How did you choose these six?"

"Our client is an extremely wealthy man with ties to the Saudi royal family. He has a preference for little girls, preferably American ones. It's funny you're here for Jordan. We looked for the other five and hand-picked them from all over the country. Jordan was handed to us. Who hired you to look for her?"

"Her Grandmother. What do you mean she was handed to you? Who in their right mind would hand their child to a creepy man who looks exactly like a murderer cum paedophile?"

"That's hurtful, Natasha. Just when I thought we were starting to get along," he tutted as he got up from the stool he had been perched on. She regretted her big mouth the moment he started walking towards her. "You hurt my feelings, you little bitch. Shall I show you how much it hurts?"

As soon as he snarled out those words he grabbed Cassandra by the hair, yanking her head forward before slamming it into the pipe she was tied against. He did it again and again until she lost consciousness.

*

Cassandra thought she had kept awake, she had tried to, but she must have blacked out for at least a second. The man was no longer trying to smash her skull open and was instead pacing somewhere in the barn. She could feel the slow drip of something running down the back of her neck. Either the back of her head was bleeding or he had managed to burst one of the pipes with her head. She guessed she was bleeding, even though the agony of her head let her believe it may well have been the latter.

Cas had tried to prepare for the worst on her way here but she had not accounted for a sick son of a bitch like this creep. The scenarios she had gone through in her head had involved violence and danger, yes, but she had not expected psychotic games with a lunatic. She kept her eyes closed for the moment – even the thought of trying to open them hurt. Her head was pounding. She could hear him pacing and mumbling but he was too quiet for her to make out his words. She strained her ears to try, but she didn't need to – suddenly his footsteps came closer and the mumbling turned into shouting.

"If it'd been up to Jackson, you would've been dead by now, you little cunt. Creep, huh? You haven't seen how much of a creep I can be. I was trying to be nice by letting you live. Maybe I should just kill you now. All I wanted was for you to know what you were stupid enough to die for. I'm not the paedo or the murderer. You asked who would hand over their child to a man like me? I think you'll find the answer interesting. The girl's own mother, that's who. Bitch sold her only daughter to us for a bit of cash. That's a bit low even for me, but I'm not complaining, that little girl is gonna make us rich. Stupid bitch of a mother would have a fit if she knew how much we were getting compared to what we gave her!

"So who's the idiot now, Detective? You may have been able to find us, but we knew you were on the property the second you stepped foot on it. We would have been celebrating our soon-to-be riches now, except for you ruining a perfectly good night. CUNT," he punctuated with kicking her hip as hard as he could. Cassandra winced at the pain but otherwise did not react. He left her, muttering to himself all the while.

Surely that couldn't be true? Did Carrie give Jordan to them for money? How could anyone do such a thing? Cas's head hurt so much she couldn't even think. It wasn't important just now. All she knew was that she needed to escape. She kept her eyes shut and kept her breathing even, in hopes that he would think that she was passed out again. She listened to the sound of his muttering getting quieter and the sound of his heavy footsteps moving away, but he only moved to somewhere else in the barn. Cas waited.

*

It felt like an hour must have passed but the man was still there. All Cassandra could hear was his nails tapping on the stool he must have been sitting on. Just tap, tap, tap. Tap, tap, tap.

The noise was starting to drive her insane. She almost considered opening her eyes and mouth to stop him but fortunately thought better of it. Her head would not have been able to cope with more trauma. The wound on the back of her head was so painful it felt like he had cracked her skull.

Cas's thoughts wandered off until suddenly she heard a lot of noise outside the barn. Gunshots. Two loud cracks followed by a series of a half-dozen more muffled shots. *What was going on?* It was still again and Cas tried to quiet her own breathing to hear, but her heart was beating faster and faster. Then came a familiar screeching noise. Her eyes opened instantly before she could stop herself. With the bright floodlights, it took a couple of moments until she was able to see properly again but when she could, she could see the noise had been the sound of the wheels of the barn door. She could see the creep had risen from his seat, eyes wary and shifting, a piece of lead pipe in his hand. Probably the same one he had knocked her out with when she had first entered the building. That felt like a lifetime ago now.

She watched him change his grip on the pipe as he walked slowly, silently, forward until he was positioned behind the gazebo wall. Then she heard it: footsteps – footsteps that sounded familiar, so inherently familiar that she didn't stop to question how or why or whether it was possible. She just shouted at the top of her lungs.

"WATCH OUT! HE'S BEHIND THE WALL!"

23

Markus slowly approached the barn in front of him. He had raced here as fast as he could after speaking to AJ, who had contacted Markus the minute it became official, if not common news. The President was going to be impeached. The mission was aborted and his days as a secret service agent were over before they had even properly begun. His disappointment at not getting to work in the White House must have been obvious but he quickly forgot about all that once AJ filled him in on what Cassandra had been up to. AJ sounded concerned, worried even. Nothing else mattered at that point. He left the training centre in such a big rush he didn't even say goodbye to anyone.

Within a matter of minutes he was racing from the James J. Rowley Training Center to Hammonton. He managed to convince a taxi driver to let him actually take his cab, claiming he needed to reach the side of his dying wife. The taxi driver agreed – in exchange for a hefty cheque of course. The ten thousand dollar cheque was probably more than the old piece of junk was worth in the first place.

Markus now found himself creeping through a farmyard and wondered what the hell Cassandra had got herself into. He was just about to investigate the bright glow of lights coming from inside the barn when he was stopped in his tracks by a loud *CRACK*. He felt – more than he heard – the whistle and rush of air just inches from his face. Someone was shooting at him.

He threw himself behind the Cadillac in the yard and looked behind him using the side view mirror. The farmhouse was positioned perfectly for someone wanting to take out an intruder on the property. Thank God that someone was a lousy shot. As he waited, he could see the shooter was aiming from an open downstairs window. Another crack. It was definitely the sound of a hunting rifle – used by someone who Markus doubted had ever been hunting before. Markus counted himself in and then quickly crouched over the hood of the car, emptying half his magazine towards the open window in rapid fire.

He heard a noise sounding like a muffled yelp and then nothing else. He wasn't sure where he had hit them but they were down. At least for now.

He took a breath and scanned the rest of the yard. He had been careless thus far in his hurry to get here. He was so close though, he could feel it. It was quiet again, there didn't seem to be anyone else here.

Markus approached the barn once again, pushed the sliding door open and made his way inside.

*

"WATCH OUT! HE'S BEHIND THE WALL!"

Cassandra. Markus spun around and ducked. Just in time. The creep had the heavy lead pipe in his hand and he was aiming for his head. Markus grabbed onto his arm to try to block him, but the skinny man was stronger than he looked. The two struggled, both trying to gain control, the man snarling at Markus. Markus didn't think he could continue in fending him off for much longer. He kept his hold on the man and kicked out at his shins as hard as he could. The man groaned but instead of letting go of the pipe, it seemed to give him a newfound energy. He managed to rip it out of Markus's hands entirely. Markus ducked and scrambled to where he had dropped his gun. Before he could reach it, heavy lead slammed into his arm. Markus screamed.

It felt like the metal had shattered the bones of his left forearm. In the background he could hear Cas cry out in worry. He ran to the other side of the barn, ducking behind some of the old appliances that sat there, buying himself some time before the creep caught up with him, making as much noise as possible so that he couldn't pinpoint where he had gone. He had to abandon his gun still on the floor and he heard it being picked up. He just needed a minute to catch his breath. This guy was not going down as easily as planned.

"You'd better come out if you'd like a pain-free death. I promise I'll make it quick and shoot you straight through the brain," the man said with the same sick chuckle he had used with Cassandra.

Markus crept behind the piles of junk, trying to position himself so that he could surprise the man from behind. Suddenly the sound of a car engine starting made him pause.

"Oh, I don't think so, pal," the creep snarled, running towards the yard and started firing at the car he clearly believed Markus was in. The sound of car tires and the crunch of gravel indicated the car was peeling out of the drive. Still convinced Markus had made his getaway, the creep ran towards the house, shouting, "Jackson! Jo! What the hell are you two doing? He got away. We have to get out of here right now!"

Markus heard the front door of the house slam. He took the chance and ran to the gazebo as fast as he could.

"Cas! Are you okay? What the fuck has he done to them?" he asked as he took in the scene before him. He searched frantically for something to cut her ties with.

"Nothing yet. They're just asleep, drugged with Sugammadex and ketamine. Same thing that knocked me out that same night I met Carrie."

"He thinks I'm gone right now. It was his accomplice that took off – that Jackson or Jo that he was shouting to.

Idiot was shooting at his mate the whole time.

"Cas, get the girls out of here," he said, having finally managed to free her with a rusty saw. "I'll go and return this little gift," he said, holding up his wrecked arm. It didn't look good. His hand was floppy and looked barely attached. Markus grabbed a golf club from the piles of junk and headed towards the house.

*

As soon as Markus left, Cas began trying to move the girls. They felt just as floppy as Markus's hand had looked. The drugs made them look as if they were dead. If their little bodies hadn't still been warm, Cas would have thought the creep had lied. It was when she was carrying the third girl to one of the trucks outside that she realised how incredibly similar they were. Someone had gone to a lot of effort to find children that looked like they shared the same blood.

*

"Joanne, he's dead!" the man cried out when he heard the front door.

He was crouching beside the body that was lying on the floor between the window and a big wooden desk. Markus had managed to hit the shooter in the neck without even being able to see him.

"What the fuck?!" The man finally looked up and, seeing it was Markus, grabbed the gun and started shooting erratically. Markus immediately dove back into the hall. He waited behind the wall for what he knew was coming. It was his gun and he had already emptied half of the chamber before. Now the man was shooting without restraint. *Twelve. Thirteen, fourteen. Fifteen.*

Click...Click. The idiot had wasted the last bullets standing between himself and Markus breaking his arms.

Markus slowly walked out from behind the wall. Not in his mind, the man jumped up from Jackson's body and launched himself at Markus. It was not what Markus was expecting. The man managed to grab Markus's wounded arm and twisted it behind his back. Markus gasped and groaned, falling to his knees on the floor.

He hadn't been expecting the man to be sharp enough to go straight for that arm. As soon as he realised that his opponent was out for blood and was happy to fight dirty, he decided to do the same. He jabbed his fingers in the man's eyes with as much force as he could muster and gouged at them.

The pain made the creep let go of Markus's arm and he scrambled to the other side of the room, grabbing a vase from the desk to hurl at Markus.

Markus dodged the vase just in time and grabbed a small statue to do the same but instead of waiting to see if it would connect, he hurled himself at the man as well, aiming for where he hoped the man would be as he ducked the projectile. He tackled him to the floor.

Legs straddled over him, he put his cold hands around his throat and squeezed. Markus kept squeezing as the man tried to struggle free. The noises coming out of the man's mouth would have turned the stomachs of most people. He was near the end. Markus could feel it. The veins in his neck started pulsing and his face was turning purple. Blood was desperately trying to find a way to his brain but Markus did not let it. He was going to kill him. He was going to kill the creep who had hurt the woman he loved.

Somehow, with a sudden burst of desperate energy, the man grabbed at the statue Markus had thrown at him. With one last attempt to save his life, he swung the statue hard against Markus's temple. It knocked Markus out instantly.

The man gasped frantically for air, his arms and legs still jerking from his near-death experience. For a couple of minutes they both lay there, recovering.

When Markus came to a moment later, the man was crawling away from him. He tried to get up but realised all he would do was faint if he did. Markus pulled himself towards the couch to hide and take cover. He could hear that the crawling had turned into a stilted walk. The footsteps made him nervous. He had to get his act together and get up from this floor. He put his hands on the floor to push himself up and immediately winced when he realised he was putting weight on his injured arm. He was about to try again when he felt a sharp pain in his back.

Markus screamed. He screamed again when the man pulled the knife back out. The man grabbed Markus by the hair and neck, ready to slit his throat. Markus was on his knees, hands wildly grasping at the man's hold on him.

He tried doubling himself over, forcing the man to bend over him.

The sound of a shot filled the room.

The knife clattered to the floor beside him. The dead weight of the man was crushing him until Markus rolled him off. He heard someone collapse onto the couch.

"It's over," Cas said tiredly from beside him. "An ambulance is en route."

24

"Hi, Miss Connelly. My name is Ashton Brooks, I'm the Deputy Chief of the Hammonton Police Department. Can we talk? I was hoping you could shed some light on what happened at the farm," the officer asked.

Cas sat up in her hospital bed, the second time in several months that she had been made infirm by a mission. Even though he hadn't meant it literally, his words immediately brought her back to the barn and how it had felt being bound and helpless, blinded by the bright floodlights. It took her awhile to realise that he was still waiting for her to answer.

"I'm sorry. I think the blows to my head have slowed down my thought process a little. What do you want to know?"

"To be completely honest, I'm not even sure where to start. This is certainly the strangest case I've ever encountered. I may have been on the force for a while now, but Hammonton doesn't usually have that much excitement. How about you just start at the beginning?" the deputy asked.

"I can do that, Officer," Cas agreed. She knew exactly what she would tell the police and what she would keep to herself. She had told the police at the scene that she would speak to them after accompanying Markus in the ambulance.

By the time they got to the hospital, the adrenaline had worn off and her head was starting to hurt more with every move she made. The pounding was starting to become unbearable again. When she asked one of the doctors for some painkillers, they insisted on examining her first. A concussion – that was all the slimy creep had done to her. She felt guilty – Markus had not been so lucky. He needed immediate surgery. His arm was fractured in several places but that was not the doctor's main concern. The stab wound to his back had caused internal bleeding and they needed to operate. He was stable though, for the time being.

While they were waiting around for updates on Markus's condition, she had spoken to AJ about exactly what she could tell the police.

"It all began about four or five weeks ago when Jonathan and I moved to DC for his new job with the secret service.

It was exciting at first. Jonathan was off the first two weeks, so we took some time to explore and sightsee. As you can imagine, it got a little less exciting for me once he started his training at the training centre. No friends or family, no job, no hobbies…So I joined an art class at the local community centre. That's where I met Carrie Williams – Jordan's mother. After our first class together, she asked if I wanted to go for a drink. Of course I said yes – she was the first person I had really met in town. That's probably why I ignored my initial instincts and managed to become good friends with her – I do remember having a funny feeling about her at first…

"When I got home that night, I collapsed on the floor. I couldn't move my arms or my legs. I was still awake though, and could hear someone smash the glass of the door through and I could hear them moving about. It was Carrie who had drugged me at the bar. Well, I know that now… but it never crossed my mind that it could have been her. We spent hours talking and I thought we really connected," Cas stopped talking when she felt that the officer had stopped listening. He seemed more interested in his phone than her story.

"I just had a look at the police report you filed for the break-in and it doesn't mention anywhere that you were drugged. Why's that?"

Cas trained her face to look innocent and neutral. She knew exactly what was in the report Deputy Brooks was reading. AJ had taken care of everything in a matter of minutes after they had agreed on what she was going to say. The report dated back to the night of Cas's first art class, but it had only been put in the system an hour ago at most. She would just have to make him believe Natasha Connelly's story.

"I hate doctors. By the time I was able to report the break-in, I felt there was no point in seeing a doctor. I was afraid the police would send me to one if I told them."

"What happened after that night?" the deputy decided to move on. After all, he had bigger fish to fry than a simple B and E.

"I continued going to the art classes. Carrie was there every time. I thought we were starting to become real friends. I even had her and Jordan over. The day that Jordan went missing…Carrie came to the morning class late after dropping Jordan off at school. I remember her telling me about how difficult Jordan had been that morning, which was why she was later than usual. Maybe about half an hour later, she gets a call from the school checking whether she had forgotten to inform them that Jordan was going to be absent. Carrie was in a panic and rushed out of the class. I went after her and offered to drive.

"That's how this all started. We searched for Jordan at their house, at Carrie's mother's, and then at the school. There was no sign of her…My dad, he's passed now, but he was a private detective when he was alive and I think my 'detective genes' or something like that kicked in at that point. I suggested to the principal that we take a look at the school's CCTV. It was shocking. You could actually see this strange woman leading Jordan away from the playground. Carrie was upset, obviously, she was crying the entire time. I couldn't imagine what it must have felt like for a mother to watch her child be taken away. That's when I decided I would do anything I could to find Jordan for her.

"I did exactly what my dad would have done. I followed every possible lead, connected all the dots. I went to all the shops in the area with cameras to see if there was any more footage showing Jordan and the woman – Joanne I think her name is. I eventually found some that captured the van they used and the tattoos on her accomplice led me to the K&A gang in Philly. On my way there I spoke to the woman that had reported the stolen licence plates of the van and she–"

The deputy cut in. "How exactly did you know that someone had reported the plates missing? That's not readily accessible information…" he looked at her with an eyebrow slightly raised, his expression telling her that he had found something that was not quite right.

She had made a mistake and said too much. It was difficult staying on top of things with a head that felt like it was about to explode. "One of Jonathan's old police buddy's did some research for me. I just wanted to know who the car belonged to. That's when he told me the plates had been stolen. I had to beg him to give me the info… Please don't ask me who it was. He made me promise to never tell anyone," she pleaded.

For a minute, Deputy Ashton Brooks just looked at her,

clearly considering his options. Cas could feel the palms of her hands get sweaty.

"You're lucky that's not integral to what we're investigating here and that there's a much bigger crime at stake...From now on, you and I will both forget you ever spoke of this."

"That sounds good to me," she sighed, relieved. "After that, I searched for a well-connected member of the K&A, someone who would know everyone. I showed the gang member the CCTV picture I had of Joanne and told him I wanted to speak to her. Of course he denied knowing her but once I left, I could see him on the phone and I just knew it was him warning her. I waited until he was busy and snuck back into the garage, grabbed his phone, and looked at the last number he had dialled. Someone called Jo. I looked up the phone provider the number belonged to and convinced them to give me the full name." At this point, Cas kept glancing at Deputy Brooks's face. He clearly didn't like the way she had gone about things, but he was keeping silent.

"After that, it was just Google and logic. This Joanne seems to have inherited a farm seven years ago. She didn't seem to live there but it sounded like the perfect place to hold an abducted child. Stupidly, I decided to check out the place myself before calling the police...Thank God I messaged Jonathan about where I was and what was happening. I felt like the police wouldn't believe me without concrete proof that this was where Jordan was being held, so I started snooping around. I could see the woman, Joanne, through the kitchen window so I knew I was in the right place at least. It sounded like she was arguing a lot with someone else in there. They sounded really angry. I went to investigate the lights I could see in the barn but I didn't realise that someone already knew I was there and was waiting to knock me out.

"When I came to, I was tied up and my head was aching. I had found Jordan, she was there in that barn – but so were five other little girls…they looked like they were dead…" Cas didn't need to fake the emotion that crept into her voice at this point. She only had to remember that first image of the girls lying there on those stretchers, unmoving and silent.

"I thought that I could sweet-talk my captor into letting me go, but he made it very clear that I was going to die after he was done with me. He was so certain I wouldn't make it past the night that he opened up about what they were planning with the girls. He told me the girls were alive, just drugged with paralysing and sleeping agents. That was the moment a bell started ringing in my head. It sounded too similar to what had happened to me that night weeks ago. I started asking him more questions and that's when I found out that Jordan hadn't really been missing. Carrie had sold her to them willingly. That sorry excuse for a mother sold her own daughter to cover the debts she owed to the gang for her and her husband's drug habits! That entire time she'd been sobbing and

crying over her daughter – the bitch was just acting!"
Cas let her rage out for a moment. She still couldn't
understand how someone could do something that was so
atrocious. She couldn't understand how she could have
been fooled by Carrie so easily.

"Apparently the girls were ordered by some Saudi
billionaire. Like a takeaway meal. Sick fuck."

"There are a lot of sick disturbed people out there," the
officer agreed, not knowing what else to say.

"They were going to transport them as bloody cargo.
Cargo! He probably ordered six just in case one died along
the way," she sniped bitterly. She took a breath to calm
herself before continuing, "After I gave him a piece of my
mind, he grabbed me by the hair and started slamming my
head against the wall. I know I passed out, I don't know
for how long, and the next thing I know is that Jonathan's
in front of me and he frees me. He tells me to get the
girls out of there and so I carry the girls to the truck as
fast as I can. Once they're all safe, I start worrying about
Jonathan. I went into the house and almost immediately I
hear a scream. Jonathan's scream. He's doubled over and
the man who held me captive is there stabbing a knife into
his back.

"I– I didn't even think…There was a rifle lying by the
window…and Jonathan was…he couldn't– I shot him.
I killed that man," she sobbed out, putting on her finest
performance to date. Deputy Brooks said nothing. All he
did was grab her hand in a comforting gesture.

"It was self-defence," he assured her quietly. "You didn't have a choice. In fact, you saved six young lives on top of that."

"What will happen to the girls? Please promise me that bitch Carrie will never see her daughter again."

"Jordan will never have to see her again, I can promise you that. Once she is awake and healthy enough, she'll be put into foster care unless there are any family members that can take care of her. We're looking into whether her grandmother had any part in all this. Obviously, wherever she is placed will be assessed thoroughly. The other five girls will be reunited with their families once we check them out as well," he told Cas comfortingly.

"Good. What about Carrie? What will happen to her?"

"We'll take care of her. My DC colleagues are set to arrest her as soon as possible. She'll watch the rest of her life pass by from within four grey walls. We've found and arrested the woman Joanne for her part in this as well.

"Get some rest. Come to the station when you get discharged and we'll take an official statement from you, all right? With all the *relevant* details for the investigation, yeah?"

"Yeah." She acknowledged that she understood his meaning with a look. She appreciated him taking care of his own. He was a good cop, who understood that sometimes the rules needed to be bent just a little. He just didn't know she'd bent them a whole lot more than that. "Thank you, Deputy Brooks. I'll see you soon," she said as convincingly as possible.

Cas wondered whether he would still be this nice in a few days' time, when he started investigating the case properly and when he realised she was only telling him some of the story. It didn't matter – she and Markus would be long gone by then, once they made sure the police had everything they needed to convict the right people. ICU would make them disappear and Natasha Connelly and Jonathan Black would be no more.

The President had been impeached. Jordan was safe. Carrie Williams and the K&A would face justice. Markus was a little worse for wear but they were both alive. In less than a day's time, they would be on a flight back to Amsterdam, their American adventure over. It certainly had not been boring, as Cassandra had originally thought it would be.

She already had plans for the future – she would get back to full health, she would definitely buy a new mattress. She would tell Markus she loved him back. She had already decided on it, and Cassandra Young never liked straying from her plans.

Now all she had to do was go back home and explain her actions to the International Control Unit…

Printed in Great Britain
by Amazon